THE CURSE OF WIHTLEA BARROWS

A MERRYWEATHERS MYSTERY

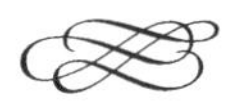

RHYS A JONES

First eBook edition published as The Dreables in 2011
By Lucky Bat Books

This edition published by Wyrmwood Books 2018
Carmarthen, SA32 8QJ, UK

This novel is entirely a work of fiction. The names, characters and incidents portrayed in it are the product of the author's imagination. Any resemblance to actual persons, living or dead, or events or localities is entirely coincidental.

A CIP catalogue record for this book is
available from the British Library

ISBN 9781999977818(paperback)
ASIN B005XEHQ4Q (e-book)

Interior Design by Polgarus Studio
Cover Design by Phil Poole

ABOUT THE AUTHOR

Rhys A Jones writes books for children. Sometimes scary, sometimes funny, always full of adventure. He was born and still lives in Wales, where he spends a lot of time in a shed in the garden making up stories. His other jobs are being a doctor, and walking the dog over the wild Welsh hills with his very understanding wife.

For more books and updates visit

www.jonestheauthor.com

twitter.com/RAJartefact

They're ancient, they're back and they're hungry.
And Sam Jones is on the menu.

Beware *The Curse of Wihtlea Barrows* and prepare to be *scary-fied.*

A Merryweathers Mystery written especially for Middle Grade readers.

Also by Rhys A Jones in the Merryweathers mysteries:

The Curse of Borage-Doone
The Curse of Ragman's Hollow

HOLIDAYS WITH GRAN

Holidays with Gran.

It was enough to make a nine-year-old weep.

You see, Sam Jones's mother had rules. Some of them were sensible, like never playing in the road, or remembering to brush your teeth night and morning. Others were understandable but not always easy to follow, like eating five pieces of fruit and vegetables a day even in national fish and chip week. But some were downright unfair – at least they were as far as Sam was concerned.

The Joneses were a pretty average family, except for the fact that Sam's mum liked exercise. Tons of exercise. So Sam swam, and ran, and played lots of games – and so did his mother and father. But Mr and Mrs Jones' favourite exercise was walking. And we're not talking about a quick stroll about the park for twenty minutes, here. These were serious, over the hills and far away, fifteen miles in an afternoon, yomps.

But Mr and Mrs Jones were kind and didn't expect Sam to do that every weekend. Not at ten years old. So they saved up their big yomps for a week's holiday in the Dolomites or on the Aztec trail in the Andes – without Sam.

Oh, they did go on holidays with Sam. Lots of nice holidays to the beach – as long as it was near a coastal path, or Middle Parks – where you had to cycle everywhere. But the yomping holiday with Sam's dad was one of Sam's mum's rules. And that was okay with Sam because yomping in the Andes wasn't quite his cup of tea, thank you very much. No, it was what he was expected to do instead that he had a problem with.

'Oh come on, Sam,' Mr Jones said as they drove down to where Granny Merryweather – she was Sam's mother's mum – lived. 'It won't be that bad. You know Gran loves having you stay and I know for a fact that she takes you to lots of great places.'

Sam was staring silently out of the car window at the blur of traffic speeding by. He hadn't said much since turning off his computer at home and trudging to the car. But Dad's coaxing stirred him out of his reverie.

'Yeah, but she can't play football anymore *and* I have to make my own bed *and* we have to talk about school and what things were like when she was a girl just after the war. She's always on about how important it is to remember something called the 'lessons of the past.' And she has even more rules than Mum does.'

'Is that where she gets it from,' his dad said with a grin.

'She's just no fun anymore, Dad,' Sam whined.

'Well, she's not as young as she was,' Mrs Jones chipped in, 'but she has lots of brilliant trips planned for you. There's that zoo and the museum.'

Sam squeezed his eyes shut. He wanted to scream out 'BOH-RING!' but with a huge effort of will, he managed to shut it off before it escaped his mouth. A part of him knew that sulking wasn't fair, and it would only make his mother and father feel guilty. But he couldn't help himself.

'It's not a zoo,' he explained through clenched teeth. 'Gran doesn't believe in zoos. It's a cat sanctuary run by her friend. She helps out on Wednesdays and last time I had to spend all day counting the tabbies. There were twenty-eight of them.'

'Wow, that must have been interesting,' Mr Jones said, trying to sound impressed.

'No, it was just bonkers because they kept hiding behind a big tree to confuse me.'

'Cats don't try and confuse you, Sam,' Mrs Jones said in a very schoolteachery way, since that was what she was when she wasn't yomping.

'Those tabbies do, I'm telling you. And it always rains. And Gran's always busy with her baking circle. Last time I had to make a Swiss roll.'

'I bet he was pretty miffed that you'd done that,' Mr Jones said, smiling in a really silly way in the rear-view mirror.

'Not funny, Dad.' Sam sighed.

'Hey, your grandmother thinks you're the best thing since sliced bread, Sam. And she'd do anything for you, you know that,' his mother reminded him, sounding more than a bit shirty.

'Yeah, but she has all these weird sayings. Like you can't go out by the back door and in through the front. And last time I was there, she bought a new broom and the first time she used it, she brushed the leaves in instead of out.'

Sam's dad made a face at his mother, who shrugged an explanation. 'It's a tradition. The broom brushes good luck in if you use it that way the first time.'

'See, Sam, it's just a tradition,' explained his father.

'And what about whistling?' Sam demanded. 'She says I should never whistle at night in case I wake something up that shouldn't be woken.'

Sam's dad paused and considered this, but all he said was, 'So maybe she's a little superstitious.'

'And you've both forgotten that time she left me at the supermarket and drove home.'

Sam's dad frowned. 'Alright, slightly weird, a tad superstitious, and a bit forgetful. But it could be worse.'

'It could be mental more like,' Sam said, feeling blood suddenly rush to his face.

Sam's mother shook her head. 'Okay, if that's how

you feel, next time you can come yomping with us,' she said stiffly. 'Only we won't be able to stop because you have a tired legs episode.'

Sam thought for a moment and then sighed. 'It would be fine if she had a DVD player or a computer or...oh, I dunno. I just wish something different would happen at Gran's for a change, that's all.'

'Maybe it will,' his dad said kindly. 'You never know. Maybe she'll ask you to make a Victoria sponge this time.'

A bit of Sam wanted to giggle then, but he stopped himself. His dad could usually make him smile but for once, Sam wanted him to know he wasn't happy.

Mum threw her husband an icy stare before deflecting it towards Sam in the rear-view. 'That's not helping, Malcolm. And Sam, stop being such a misery guts. The fact is she's not getting any younger and you're getting older. But for the next week, you'll just have to put up with each other.'

HALF AN HOUR later they arrived at Gran's. Gwladys Mary Merryweather lived in a bungalow with a paddock at the back where she kept hens. The TV was black and white and she didn't have a laptop or an iPod. But she did have lots of books and a chocolate Labrador called Troop and a snooty black cat called Ginger. Sam had asked once why Gran had called the cat Ginger and she'd said, with a completely straight face, 'Because that's what he wants to be called.'

Gran was always saying stuff like that with a completely straight face and most of the time Sam had no idea if she was joking or not. The door to the bungalow opened as they pulled up. Sam saw straight away that Gran hadn't changed. Gwladys Merryweather wasn't fat and she wasn't thin. She had hair that was halfway between silver and light blue depending on how recently she'd been to the hairdresser. She wore a flowery dress and some beads and a pair of glasses attached to a brown cord that hung around her neck so that she wouldn't lose them. The glasses looked a bit like seagull's wings.

Sam retrieved his backpack and suitcase from the car and followed his mum and dad inside. Everything was spick and span in Gran's bungalow, as indeed was Gwladys Merryweather. The living room table was laid with china cups and two three-tiered plates; one laden with small sandwiches and the other groaning under the weight of the most amazing selection of cakes.

'Vanilla custard tarts!' Sam's mum groaned and then added in awe, 'These aren't you know who's?'

Gran nodded her head and smiled. 'Brenda McPherson's very own.'

Sam's mother actually squealed and ate two, one straight after the other. Gran ate one as well and, spitting crumbs, she said, 'I have to admit that there is only one other person in the world who makes vanilla custard tarts better than Brenda McPherson.'

'Is that you, Gwladys?' asked Sam's dad with his mouth full.

'Me?' Gran said, sounding surprised. 'Oh no, I'm more an éclair specialist. No, there's a woman in the village I grew up in called Libby Brown. She makes the best vanilla custard tarts in the world.'

Mum and Gran started to make cooing noises and went on to discuss chocolate éclair league tables. Dad's eyes went up to the ceiling and it made Sam want to giggle, but, with difficulty, he stopped himself again.

'Made some fresh cream horns for you, Sam,' Gran said. 'Your favourite.'

'No thanks,' Sam said. 'Not hungry.'

'Sam, you're always hungry,' his mother said.

'No, let him be,' Gran said, eyeing Sam with that special look of hers that implied that she always knew what Sam was thinking, even when he didn't really know himself. She pursed her lips and added, 'They'll keep. If you don't want anything to eat, Samuel, you can take your bag to your room while I make a fresh pot of tea.'

Gran was the only person in the world that ever called him Samuel and when she did it usually meant she was a bit mad at him. He could have eaten two of Gran's cream horns without them touching the sides, but he didn't because he knew that if he did, he'd forget about feeling hard done by and grumpy. Gran's cakes had that effect. More than once he'd asked her what special ingredients she used to make them taste so good. Gran just peered at him through her glasses and said, 'Care, love and attention,' before turning away and adding quietly, 'and maybe a pinch of special Merry-weather spice.'

Sam's bedroom was old and had circus wallpaper featuring elephants and lions and clowns and ringmasters, which Sam had loved when he'd been younger. Now it just looked childish and tired. Gran had arranged all the things they'd found over the years together on a dressing table: Glassy smooth stones from the river and tickets to funfairs jostled with battered dinky toys that he'd loved to play with once, but which now just looked rusty and old and squeaked when he tried to run them over the doily.

As he meandered back to the living room, he glanced in to the kitchen. Gran had her back to him, one hand on a chair back for balance as she reached into the fridge for some milk. The radio was playing old songs, but as he approached the living room, he couldn't help but overhear his mum and dad speaking.

'I don't know what's happened between them,' his dad said. 'They were the best of pals once, remember? He used to cry his eyes out when we took him home.'

'Since her hip operation, she's not as agile. You can see that,' Mum replied.

'See her wince when she got up? She's still in pain,' added Dad. 'She obviously needs a bit of looking after.'

'She'll never admit to that in a million years...'

Sam hesitated. He'd never heard his mum and dad talk like this before. There was a long silence and then Dad said, 'Maybe that's it. Maybe Sam just wants the old Gran back and just can't accept that she isn't the woman she was.'

There was a rattle of cups from the corridor and Gran appeared with a new tray. A powdery smudge of icing sugar dusted one eyebrow and the tip of her nose and as usual, she smelled of cinnamon and soap. 'I see you've grown a couple of inches since Easter,' she said.

Sam shrugged. He didn't know what to say to that. The smile changed to a scowl on Gran's face. 'Well, don't just stand there like a statue, open the door.'

Sam sighed and did as he was told.

DREAMS

After they'd had tea, Sam's mum and dad left for the airport.

'Be good,' Sam's mother said after she'd hugged him for the fourth time.

'Try and enjoy yourself,' Sam's dad said with a wistful twinkle in his eye. The funny thing was that Sam's gran had a twinkle just like that when he'd been smaller and sat on her knee and looked at books about sharks and dinosaurs. But lately that twinkle seemed to be getting dimmer.

'Don't wear your legs out,' Sam called after them as they drove down the street.

When the car finally turned the corner, Sam turned and looked around from his grandmother's gate at the bungalow with a sinking heart. It was going to be a long seven days.

They always had hot chocolate just before bed. It was

one of the things he did look forward to about being at his gran's. But with the chocolate came one of Gran's little rules. She insisted on reading to him. If they didn't finish a book by the time the week was over, he'd take it with him to finish at home. But Gran liked to read books about animals and jungles and the outdoors. They were okay but what Sam really liked were books about wizards and ghosts. Gran wasn't keen on those at all.

'Can't be doing with all that silly stuff,' she'd say. 'Real life is much more interesting.' But Sam had heard her mutter under her breath, 'And anyway, there's no reason to tempt fate, if you ask me.' He had no idea what she meant by that.

The book she was reading to him now was about some children called Susan and Timmy, who camped on an island in a lake and who pretended to be pirates. There was no one in his whole school called Susan or Timmy, and Sam thought the story sounded a bit old-fashioned, just camping on an island. Still, it was quite exciting the way Gran read it. But after three chapters, Gran closed the book and looked at Sam.

'If your yawns get any bigger, you'll swallow Troop.'

'I am a bit tired,' Sam said.

'Did you read in the car on the way down? That sometimes makes you tired.'

Sam nodded.

'What were you reading?' Gran asked.

'About a boy called George whose grandmother was horrible and who was always bullying him when his parents weren't at home. The boy decided to make some special medicine for her because he was convinced she was a witch. It was a really funny book.'

'Sounds as if it wasn't good news for the grandmother,' Gran said.

'Just as well you're not a witch then, isn't it?'

'No such things as witches. Besides, I retired a long time ago.'

Sam's mouth turned into the shape it became when he wanted to laugh but nothing came out. He couldn't help but notice that Gran wasn't laughing either. He got as far as the sofa when Gran said, 'Don't I even get a goodnight kiss, then?'

Sam turned. 'Mum said that since I'm now ten I don't have to kiss people if it makes me feel uncomfortable and childish.'

'Is that what she said.' Gran's voice sounded suddenly odd and tight.

'Well, goodnight,' Sam said.

'Goodnight, Sam,' said his gran. When Sam got to his bedroom, he heard his grandmother blow her nose and sniff for quite a long time.

THAT NIGHT, as he lay in bed waiting for sleep to come, Sam thought about what he really knew about his grandmother. He knew she was old. He didn't really know what she'd been before she'd been just Gran, although he realised that she'd probably had a job once. Maybe she'd been a fireman or a nurse. Maybe a baker. He didn't think she'd been in the army or a policeperson. But the truth was he didn't really know. Just like he didn't know what was in the locked cupboard under Ginger's basket in the boxroom. When he asked Gran about that, all she'd say was,

'Things that need to be looked at when they need to be looked at and not before.'

That was classic Gran. No explanation, just some weird old saying that got you thinking all sorts of things.

What he did know was that she didn't really like football or books about wizards and ghosts and vampires and was always telling him to be polite to people even if they were nasty to you. Sam thought that was just plain silly. But Gran was insistent.

'Be nice to them. Takes the wind right out of their sails,' she'd say. 'Makes them think about what they're doing. And since most people don't think at all, it's always worth a try.'

Sam couldn't see the point of it. But then he couldn't see the point of making his bed every day or making sure the fireguard was always in place at night even when there wasn't a fire.

'Never know what might try and come down that chimney,' Gran explained.

And then of course there was broccoli. He couldn't see the point of broccoli at all. But it, along with the fireguard and bed making, was a big part of being at

Gran's. Sam turned over. His foot was itching, and he had to reach down to scratch it. He wished he'd eaten those cream horns now too since his stomach was rumbling incessantly.

But it wasn't cream horns Sam dreamed of that night. Instead, he dreamed of being on top of a mountain with his mother and father: They were on a high trail with the world stretched out like a green chess board beneath them. But he was way behind and much as he tried, he couldn't seem to get his parents' attention. Even if he ran he couldn't seem to catch up. In the end, they disappeared out of sight and Sam was alone in that high place.

Way down below he could see Gran's bungalow with Troop barking. Slowly he made his way down the mountain towards it. But when he was halfway down, a mist came down out of nowhere and engulfed him. It was a cold and damp mist that seemed to suck the heat out of his bones and he began to shiver. Worse, inside the mist he had no idea of direction or time and all he could do was wander around the mountainside. From somewhere a long way away he thought he could hear Troop barking. But there were other things in the mist too. Whispering things that came and went and sometimes he thought he could feel the touch of very cold fingers on his face. He was very tired but he knew that sleeping on the mountainside in the mist wasn't a good idea. He tried to listen for Troop's bark and walked towards it. He seemed to walk for ages. Finally, he got too tired and sat down on the cold mountainside. Maybe it would be okay for him to close his eyes and rest for a moment or two.

Then he felt something warm and wet touch his hand. He leapt up. A big furry head nudged his leg and something wet flicked at his fingers…and, as was the way with dreams, Sam woke up. He was in his bed at Gran's bungalow and Troop was there licking his outstretched hand. Sam didn't know quite why but he was suddenly really glad that Troop had come to wake him up. He got up and dressed and looked out of the window.

It wasn't raining.

But it was Wednesday.

Sam groaned.

THE CAT SANCTUARY

The cat sanctuary was, as usual, full of cats. It was run by Mrs Walpole, who wore a fur-splattered pink sweatshirt and jeans even on the hottest summer day and had wispy hair that was always falling into her eyes. Sam couldn't decide if the lipstick she wore was an even brighter shade than her sweatshirt.

'Hello Sam,' she said as he opened the door of Gran's battered estate car. 'How lovely to see you again. Did I ever tell you that your eyes are exactly the same shade as Bugle's? He was one of my favourite Siamese. And your hair is still as black as Ginger's.' She beamed at Sam, who pretended his seat belt was stuck to avoid being hugged by Mrs Walpole. But he managed to compress his lips into a toothless smile in return. Out of the corner of his eye he thought he could see Gran watching him.

'Oh Gwladys,' Mrs Walpole fussed. 'There was no

need for you to have come in today. Not when you have guests.' She sent a second beaming smile towards Sam. He slitted his eyes to deflect it.

'Nonsense,' said Gran, already rolling up her sleeves. 'Sam loves it here, don't you, Sam?'

'Well, actually—' Sam began to say. He was cut off in mid-reply by Mrs Walpole.

'The cats certainly seem to like him, I know that.' She put her hands on her hips and snorted. 'Always a good sign in my book.' She snorted again. It sounded like a horse whinnying.

'Now then, Alicia,' Gran said, 'let's get on with the muckings.'

Sam watched as Mrs Walpole led Gran up a paved area between the cattery cages. There were a hundred cats at the sanctuary and that meant a hundred cats to clean up after every day. Sam had once been to see the muckings and had absolutely no wish to see them ever again. He certainly had no desire to watch someone shovelling them into bags for disposal.

He shuddered at the memory and proceeded to head in the opposite direction towards a meadow at the side of the cattery. The first of the cats started to follow him after he'd gone perhaps ten yards. Others joined from all over the cattery. By the time he'd reached the edge of the meadow, there were thirty cats following him. When he got to the old threshing machine that sat rusting like the brown skeleton of some ancient dinosaur in one corner of the field, there were at least fifty cats behind him.

Sam stopped and turned to confront them. When he stopped walking so did they. He had no idea what they wanted, and it had been the same last year and the year before. A plague of cats wherever he went.

'Shoo,' Sam said, waving his arms about. The cats watched his arms but didn't move. Instead they meowed and swished their tails.

'Go away,' Sam ordered.

The cats ignored him.

Sighing and shaking his head, Sam sat with his back towards the wheel rim of the old threshing machine and began plucking at blades of grass and daisies, one eye on the cat entourage. One by one, realizing that Sam was not on the move any more, they sat and began preening themselves or licking their paws as cats do.

Sam wasn't scared of cats; in fact, he quite liked them. Not as much as dogs, which were his favourite animal, but even Ginger, who was a pretty independent cat who didn't like a lot of fondling, would rub against him at the breakfast table every morning and that was okay. At home the Joneses didn't have any pets. It decreased the chances of 'catching parasites,' or so Sam's mum said.

Sam turned his eyes up towards the sky. The sun was warm and mellow on his face and the aroma of new-mown hay drifted over in wafts from the farm next door. Insects buzzed between the buttercups and campions, and barely moving cotton wool clouds hung high overhead. Sam made himself comfortable and tried to see what shapes the clouds were making. He saw a hen's head and a cricket bat and an eagle's wing. He made chains out of the daisies and played a game of throwing pebbles into an old bucket as the cats watched lazily. At midday, he and the cats plodded back to the reception office, where Gran and Mrs Walpole were waiting. Mrs Walpole was grinning.

'Did you have a nice time with the cats, Sam?' she asked.

'They keep spying on me,' Sam said.

'Yes. Quite extraordinary that. They don't bother with anyone else.'

'Hmph,' Sam grunted.

Mrs Walpole beamed. 'You're like your gran. She has a way with animals too and she's so kind and generous with her time. I expect you two get up to all sorts.'

Sam thought about harrumphing again but decided against it.

'WHY DO those cats keep following me every time I go there?' Sam asked as they set off in Gran's car.

'Perhaps it's because they like you,' Gran said.

'Well, I don't like it when they follow me.'

'Now why doesn't that surprise me,' Gran said, her eyes narrowing in a dangerous way. 'You know what, Samuel? Animals don't need your approval to admire and like you.'

'I didn't ask them to like me,' Sam said. 'That's not fair.'

'Fair doesn't come into it. Unconditional love, it's called. Dogs and cats and mums and dads and *grandparents* have it by the bucket load.'

'Sounds pants to me,' Sam mumbled. He didn't like it when Gran was like this. The things she said made him think too much.

'Yes, well,' Gran said, 'pants it may be to you, but not to the cats. In fact, I've noticed that quite a few things are pants to you these days. Especially when it comes to doing things you don't want to do. You know, most people have things they don't really want to do but they end up doing them anyway because they're necessary. Duty, it's called. And doing it with good grace is the trick. But I expect you're a bit too young to know that, even if you are old enough to not let people kiss you goodnight because it makes you feel uncomfortable.' Gran shifted in her seat and sighed. 'Now then, what do you want to do? The museum has a new exhibition of volcanic rocks. Or there's the garden centre.'

'Do we have to?' Sam protested.

Gran shot him a withering glance. When she spoke, it was in a slow and deliberate voice. 'No, we don't *have* to. But we need to do something because you have a face like a slapped bottom and I don't think I can stand a week of looking at it.'

'But it's so boring, Gran.'

'How can you say that? The sun is shining, we're free to go wherever we like. Use your imagination.'

'Can't we do something else, like go to the pictures? There's a new scary one out about a secret castle and an ogre and...'

'That'll be quite enough of that,' Gran said, pursing her lips. 'I have no control over what your mother and father let you watch but here, with me, there'll be none of that.'

'But why?' Sam asked.

'Because,' Gran said, and Sam could see that her knuckles had turned white on the steering wheel. 'That's why.'

Sam turned his face away and slumped in the passenger seat. He looked out of the window at all the boring fields and the cows and the sheep. Where were the ghouls and the monsters and the fantastic castles of his dreams when he needed them?

But he had no time to dwell on those thoughts. Suddenly, the car started to sputter and start like a stuttering kangaroo. Sam heard Gran sigh.

'That's just what we don't need,' she said and pulled over into a convenient lay-by.

'What is it?' Sam asked. The car was making strange hissing noises. Gran leaned forward with her glasses on her nose and tapped a dial on the dashboard.

'Engine temperature's in the red. Looks like we've got a leaky radiator.'

She got out of the car and Sam followed. Instantly,

Sam felt the sun bake through his T-shirt. Gran fiddled with the bonnet and in a jiffy had it held open on a metal strut. A low whistling sound emerged from a thin, square block of metal at the front of the car.

'Stand back,' Gran ordered. She took out a handkerchief and used it to grab hold of the radiator cap and slowly unscrewed it. The hissing noise got louder until eventually, steam started pouring out.

'There,' said Gran, 'that should stop it from blowing up at least...'

She got no further. As Sam and his grandmother watched the steam got thicker and started to billow out, not in a thin stream, but in great thick folding clouds. Within half a minute, they were completely enveloped. The steam, if that is what it was, was so thick, they couldn't even see the car.

It was then that Sam heard the voice. It sounded like it was coming from behind them. They both turned and looked. It was like staring at a miniature film screen. The image distorted and shifted in the steam, but it was clear enough to make out that the voice belonged to a girl. She stood near some trees and looked to be no more than eight or nine. Long plaits hung down her back and she kept glancing nervously over her shoulder. She rubbed her palm over a pebble held in her other hand as she spoke.

Watcher, Watcher, wherever you be,
Over land or over sea,
As you are bound then so are we.

Gran made a weird sort of choking noise in her throat. The girl looked up. She seemed to be looking directly at Sam and at Gran.

'They're loose, Mother Merryweather. The Dreables are loose and bad things are coming. Please help us. Please.'

A sudden gust of arctic wind seemed to whip up from nowhere and Sam was sure he felt the sting of ice on his cheeks for a second. Then the steam was gone, ripped apart by the unnatural breeze.

'Wow,' Sam said. 'What was that?'

But his grandmother didn't answer. Gwladys Merryweather was as white as sheet and was trembling.

'Gran?' Sam asked. 'Are you alright?'

'No,' answered Gran in a shaky whisper. 'I am not alright. I'm as not alright as I'll ever be. I never thought it would happen after all this time, never.'

'What would happen?'

Gran seemed to come back to herself then. Her eyes refocused and her expression moulded itself into a normal looking Gran face.

'That radiator. Never thought it would boil over like that,' she said unconvincingly.

'But the girl. What about the girl?'

'Come on, Samuel,' Gran said, screwing back the radiator cap. 'Get back into the car. I have things to do.'

Sam did as he was told, his brain on fire with questions. The car started first time. Gran turned on the radio really loudly and didn't say anything on the way

and neither did Sam. He knew from the expres-
n her face that she wouldn't tell him anything. He sat and thought and tried to imagine just what exactly a Dreable might be.

Use your imagination, his Gran was always saying. So he did, and it was almost making him burst with inquisitiveness.

MRS. WALPOLE'S CHERRY BAKEWELLS

Gran drove home at twice the speed she normally drove at. This was also extremely weird because Gran didn't usually like to rush. Once before while driving home at Gran's usual pace of twenty-nine miles an hour, Sam had looked around in response to a beeping horn to see a man in the car behind shaking his fist at him and pointing at his watch. When the man eventually overtook them, Gran smiled and waved at the man in her *'be polite even when they're nasty'* way. The man had not waved back, but his face had been the colour of a ripe aubergine. He'd looked as if he'd wanted to shout something and seeing Gran's polite smile had made his eyes bulge and his face turn even more purple than it had been before. But in the end, the aubergine-faced man did nothing except speed off with an expression akin to someone that had just bitten into a sherbet lemon only to find that it was full of real lemon juice.

When they arrived back at Gran's bungalow, she took off her coat and turned to Sam. 'Right, I've got some important things to do, so why don't you watch TV and I'll put a pizza in the oven for you.'

Sam couldn't believe his ears.

'But it's only one o'clock,' he spluttered.

'And?' Gran said as if midday TV and pizza was a normal lunchtime offering.

'But you never let me watch telly in the daytime,' persisted Sam.

'Well, today is different,' Gran said.

'What about the museum?'

'You hate the museum.'

'But you said pizza.'

'Samuel, do you or don't you want to watch TV and eat pizza?' Gran said, sounding exasperated.

'Yes,' said Sam quickly before she could change her mind.

He flicked through the channels on Gran's ancient TV and managed to find a cartoon as he munched on the pizza. When the cartoon finished, all he could find was news so he turned the TV off. On the shelf next to the table with the reading lamp was an encyclopaedia. Sam had to stand on the chair to reach it, but he managed to get it down. Outside the window, thick grey clouds began to boil up from the west as Sam sat with the book on his knees thumbing through the pages. There was nothing about Dreables.

From somewhere in the bungalow, he could hear lots of mutterings and banging. Sam creaked the living room door open and peeked out. Gran was bustling about, carrying clothes into her bedroom and talking to herself.

'Never thought…never thought it would happen…. Dreables…after all this time, Dreables, I ask you…'

Ginger walked past, hesitated, and looked at him.

Sam whispered, 'Go away,' and shut the door again quickly. He didn't want Ginger purring and rubbing his back all over his legs just now. It was too distracting. He waited a few seconds for the cat to get fed up before opening the door once more. Gran was walking towards the box room. Sam crept out and went into his bedroom. From there, with the door ajar, he could see into the box room quite easily. What he saw now was Gran's bottom as she leaned over and unlocked the cupboard. He couldn't quite see around the expanse of flowery fabric, but he guessed that she was pulling something out. Sam heard the click of metal clasps. Gran muttered again as she rummaged. Something clattered to the floor and Gran said, 'Damn and blast.'

Then she was scooping things up and Sam heard the clasps click shut. Gran stood up and half turned. She was holding a small but battered leather suitcase. He saw a blur of flowery patterns as she hurried past. Sam waited and then crept across to the box room. He got down onto the floor and reached under the cupboard. His hand felt something cold and metallic and he brought it out into the light. It was a coin. But not like any he'd ever seen before. It was dull and worn and had a very small hole near one edge, like it might have been strung as a pendant. He could see the shape of someone's head on one side, but it was indistinct. He went back into his bedroom and sat on his bed looking at the coin. He sat there for ages, lost in thought. But then he heard Gran approaching and had just about time to thrust the coin into his jeans pocket before she opened the door and came in looking harassed.

'Right. Had enough to eat?'

Sam nodded.

'Good. Have to go back to Mrs Walpole's. Come on.'

The car was much fuller than usual, partly because Troop and Ginger were in the boot but also because the back seat had been piled up with things covered by an old blanket.

'Where's all this stuff going to, Gran?' Sam asked.

'Business,' Gran said.

'Has it got anything to do with what happened this afternoon?'

Gran looked as if she'd just swallowed a snail.

'What happened this afternoon?' Gran asked.

'You know. The car and all that steam and that little g –'

'No,' Gran said hurriedly, 'that was just a –'

'Really weird thing wasn't it?' Sam said, unable to keep the excitement out of his voice.

Gran opened her mouth and then shut it again, twice. She kept her eyes on the road and wouldn't look at Sam. Finally, she swallowed and said,

'Because I've got some business to attend to out of town, Mrs Walpole has agreed to let you stay for a while.'

'WHAT?' yelled Sam. 'But Mrs Walpole doesn't do anything except look after cats. She smells of cats. Her whole house smells of cats.'

Gran was shaking her head. 'It's a cattery. Of course it's going to smell of cats. But the last time I checked, a bit of cat smell never killed anyone. And for your information, Mrs Walpole was once a matron at one of the biggest children's hospitals in the country. I can't think of anyone better qualified to look after a child, can you?'

Sam slumped in his seat, stung by what Gran had said. He wanted to yell at her that he wasn't a child and that he could look after himself, but he knew it would do no good. She'd never allow him to stay in the bungalow on his own for even an hour.

'It's just for a day, two at the most,' Gran added after a while.

'But what am I going to do at Mrs Walpole's?' Sam protested.

'You could help with the cats.'

'I don't want to help with the cats. She might make me do the muckings.'

'She won't.'

'How do you know? This isn't fair. I'm supposed to be on holiday with you.'

'I know, Sam,' said Gran, and she sounded suddenly genuinely regretful. 'It's just that something has come up and it can't wait.'

'Why can't I come with you?'

'You can't. It's not s…it's not possible.'

Sam frowned. For one minute there, it had sounded suspiciously like Gran was going to say 'not safe.' 'Why are Troop and Ginger in the car? Are they going with you?'

'Yes, but…'

'Oh, so it's okay for a cat and a dog but not for me? That's just not fair.'

Gran looked across at him, but she wasn't angry anymore. 'Things aren't always fair in this world, Sam. It's about time you realised that. I'll make it up to you, I promise, but there's nothing to discuss. I've made my mind up.'

WHEN THEY GOT to the cattery, Sam got out of the car and was immediately surrounded by a dozen cats that started meowing and rubbing against his shoes and squeezing themselves between his legs as he tried to walk.

'Get off,' Sam said as he almost tripped. He shot Gran an accusing stare. 'See, I can't stay here. These cats are all mental.'

'They just like you.'

'They don't even know me,' Sam whinged.

'Cats are very mysterious creatures at the best of times, Samuel. Maybe they like you because of something you've done in the past, or maybe even yet to do.'

'If I stay here, they might all gang up on me more like,' Sam argued, not really listening.

Just then Mrs Walpole appeared in her pink sweatshirt. 'Oh Gwladys,' she said, 'I see you've brought Sam. Everything is arranged.' She brushed hair from her eyes and looked a bit flushed.

'I am so grateful for you having him like this, Alicia,' Gran said, 'but I can't stop to chat. I must be getting on.'

'Oh, but I have some cherry Bakewells just about to come out of the oven,' said Mrs Walpole.

Gran, who had seemed to be most anxious to leave, suddenly had a severe case of the second thoughts. 'Really?' she said. 'Not your special cherry Bakewells with extra almonds and icing?'

'The very same.' Mrs Walpole smiled. 'I thought you might like some for the journey.'

'You shouldn't have,' said Gran, following Mrs Walpole into the house.

Sam was still fuming over Gran rushing off like this. All sorts of thoughts and feelings were bubbling up in his head. A truculent bit of him was glad that she was going because it hadn't been very much fun being with Gran that day. At least with Mrs Walpole he might be allowed to do what he wanted – as long as it was to do with cats. But then another part of him felt strangely anxious. He had no idea why for quite some time – until his mother's overheard words popped into his head again.

'She's not as young as she was… She's still in pain…. She obviously needs a bit of looking after.'

What if something happened to Gran? What if she went somewhere and fell over and broke her other hip? What would his mother and father say about him then? Sam pondered that thought, and in the process, had an idea. He was never sure where exactly it came from, but like most brainwaves, it was there in his head in an instant.

'I'm going to the meadow,' he said loudly in his best grumpy voice.

'Okay, Sam,' sang Mrs Walpole over her shoulder. 'Tea is at five.'

But Sam didn't head for the meadow. He waited until both women were out of sight and tiptoed towards Gran's car. He opened the back door and heard Troop whine a welcome.

'Shh,' Sam said as he swiftly arranged some old coats of Gran's on the floor between the front and back seat and lay down. Quickly he pulled down the edge of the blanket that was covering whatever Gran had loaded the car up with so that it covered him too. He made himself comfortable and waited. He'd just settled when he noticed the racket. It sounded like twenty cats meowing at the same time very close by.

'Oh no,' groaned Sam.

He scrambled up on to his knees and peered out of the back seat window. Yes, just as he'd feared, twenty-five cats sat outside the car, meowing to their hearts' content. Sam waved his arms and hissed, 'Get lost,' through the glass, but this just seemed to make the meowing louder.

Desperate now, Sam opened the back door carefully and in a loud whisper said,

'Leave me alone. You'll give the game away.'

The cats stopped meowing.

'Look,' Sam said, 'I'm glad you like me alright, but if you all stay there, Gran and Mrs Walpole will know I'm here. Something's up. Something really weird and I don't know if Gran can sort it out on her own. So I'm going to find out what it is, okay?'

To Sam's utter amazement, as one the cats turned tail and sashayed off towards the meadow just as Sam heard Gran and Mrs Walpole's voices emerging from the direction of the house. He ducked back down and pulled over the blanket.

'These smell gorgeous, Alicia,' Gran said.

'Can't get them any fresher,' Mrs Walpole said. 'And

don't worry about Sam, he'll be fine. You never know, he might even help out with the muckings.' Mrs Walpole let out one of her whinnying laughs.

Sam was bitterly disappointed not to hear Gran protest.

LIBBY BROWN

The journey seemed to take forever. There was something hard on the floor of the car that felt like an iron bar in the small of Sam's back and which prevented him from getting too comfortable. But he was determined to stay quiet and still. Occasionally he risked a glimpse of the outside world as they sped along. All he could see from where he lay were the tops of trees and sometimes a glimpse of blue as a motorway sign flashed by. But there was nothing that helped him work out where they were going.

The radio played songs that Sam had never heard, and sometimes Gran hummed or sang along. Finally, after several hours, the car slowed down and he was rolled from side to side as they started to take some serious bends. Then they climbed for what seemed like an age before, quite abruptly, the car came to a full stop.

The thing that struck Sam more than anything was

the sudden silence. Up to that point there had been the whooshing of other cars and the drone of the engine and the tinny music from the radio, but now there was absolutely nothing. No wind, no other cars, no birds. Nothing, except the occasional metallic click of the cooling engine. He heard the front door open and the series of small puffs and groans that Gran always made getting in or out of the car. He waited for an 'Ooh, me poor joints,' and was a bit disappointed when it didn't come.

He heard the door shut again and once more there was a dead silence. Sam pulled down the blanket and looked up. Outside the window there was nothing. No shapes or shadows, just a dense white mist that swirled and billowed. It seemed to Sam that it wasn't dissimilar to the stuff that had poured out of the engine when they'd stopped that morning. He struggled up onto one knee to look out between the front seats. There, just in front of the bonnet of the car, was Gran. She was waving her arms about like those people he'd seen on TV at race courses that took bets. The only difference was that Gran looked like a demented one, and Sam thought he could hear her chanting too. But then, something truly extraordinary happened. Gran took a deep breath and began to blow out air.

The mist in front of her began to clear away as if it was being burned, writhing and retracting like the tentacles of some huge octopus. It left a clear gap in the fog. Still Gran continued to blow and still the gap continued to clear and Sam saw the road ahead revealed. They were on a single track on a moor with nothing but grass on either side. Grass and then the mist. After a whole minute of blowing, Gran stopped to catch her breath and leaned on the bonnet for support. Sam ducked down again just in time because a second later, Gran got back into the car and started the engine. The car moved forward slowly negotiating more bends until finally they started descending.

But Sam wasn't thinking about the journey anymore; his heart was racing too quickly. There was no doubting what he'd seen with his own eyes. Gran had just done something – something weird – and the mist had just melted away. But what exactly had she done? Called up the wind? Cast a spell? He shook his head. Gran, his Gran, didn't do stuff like that. His brain boiled with unanswered questions as he lay under the blanket. Eventually the road began to flatten out once more until finally they came to a full stop. Gran got out. This time she left the door open and Sam risked another peek. Outside, the mist had gone and through the side window, he could see a stone cottage surrounded by an overgrown garden. His grandmother was at the door of the cottage, trying to get a stubborn key to fit, muttering to herself as she shoved at the door with her shoulder.

Sam saw his chance. Quietly, he eased open the back door on the side away from the cottage and backed out, keeping nice and low. His knees were really stiff after the journey and he desperately wanted to stand up, but he daren't. He hid behind the rear of the car, one eye on Gran, as he took in his surroundings. The cottage nestled on a hillside overlooking a neat village. A row of small houses and cottages lined a curving street. Behind, the landscape was made up of a series of regular mounds of small hills dotted with copses and ferns. It reminded Sam of the lid of the box of chocolates Gran gave Mrs Walpole for Christmas every year.

He glanced again at Gran. She didn't look any different, but Sam was seeing her in a different way. A what-exactly-is-she-going-to-do-now kind of way. He was half expecting her to mutter an incantation and blow the front door off its hinges, but all she did was force the cottage door open with her shoulder, and suddenly she was coming back down the path. Sam ducked even lower and eased his way around the back of the car.

Gran went to the rear door and pulled off the blanket and started to grab the boxes of provisions she'd loaded. Sam waited until Gran's head was buried in the car. He sprinted low for the cottage garden and hid behind a large bush. He squatted there while Gran took in one load of stuff and, just after she passed him on the way back out to the car, slipped in through the cottage door like a thief. He was expecting to have to dash around trying to find somewhere to hide, but to his utter astonishment, he saw that inside the cottage was exactly like Gran's bungalow: same furniture and decorations, same living room and kitchen, and even the same layout in his bedroom.

'How weird is that?' he said to himself. He ran into the living room and ducked behind a sofa and watched as Gran completed her removals. He couldn't stay in the living room, that was clear, but since Gran had no idea he was there, the most obvious place to hide would be in the last place she'd look; his bedroom.

Sam waited until Gran went out for another load and then hurried to the room opposite the box room. Inside, it had an unmade bed and the drawers and wardrobe were just the same as in the bungalow. Except, of course, none of his things were in the drawers. But the bed did have an eiderdown which hung over the sides just enough to hide someone lying beneath. That was where Sam secreted himself. He could hear Gran's to-ing and fro-ing, but his mind was racing as he tried to work out just what was going on. Why did Gran have a cottage in the middle of nowhere set out in exactly the same way as her bungalow? And how could she blow a passage through the mist like she had done on the moor? It didn't make any sense at all. He heard Troop's paws pad along the passageway and felt a cold nose on his leg.

'Go away, Troop,' Sam said. 'You'll give the game away.'

But Troop just wagged his tail and sniffed, got bored and padded off somewhere else. Then Ginger came in and meowed for a while, but then he went away too. Shortly after, Sam heard Gran mumble and groan and the door to the bedroom flew open. But all he heard after that was the twang of the springs as Gran dumped something heavy on the bed before shuffling off.

Lying on the floor of the car for hours had not been very comfortable. But under the bed, there was a warm carpet. Sam must have dozed off because the next thing he remembered was the noise of the doorbell. He wiped a dribble of saliva from the corner of his mouth and crept out from under the bed to peek through the open door. Troop and Ginger were sitting in the passageway watching the door avidly. Gran appeared from the living room.

'Coming,' she said and opened the door.

Silhouetted against the late afternoon light was a big woman. She was taller than Gran and much rounder. She had grey hair and glasses and seemed to be smiling a lot.

'Libby Brown,' Gran exclaimed. 'This is a surprise.'

Troop began to growl low in his throat.

'Ah,' said Libby Brown. 'I see you've brought the animals.'

'Just the two. Troop, hush now. Don't know what's got into him, I really don't.'

Sam looked at Troop. His ears were back, and he didn't look at all pleased. Ginger's fur looked like it was a dish of iron filings recently exposed to a magnet.

'Been cooped up in the car for hours. Ignore them,' added Gran. 'Come in, come in.'

Sam wanted to shout out to Gran and say no, don't let

her in. Because he, like Troop and Ginger, didn't like the way Libby Brown was smiling. At least her mouth was smiling, but her eyes weren't. They looked sharp and calculating. And his and the animals' instincts were proved alarmingly correct by something Libby Brown did as she followed Gran into the kitchen. At the very last moment, when Gran was through the door and unable to see Libby, the big woman turned her face towards Troop and Ginger and it transformed into something ghastly. It was like the worst Halloween mask Sam had ever seen. From that horrible face protruded a tongue. And the worst of it was, the tongue looked as if it was dark blue.

Troop whined, and Ginger hissed.

'Nice,' Sam said quietly to himself once the tingling in his spine had faded.

Libby Brown had one of those voices that could carry though a thunderstorm. He didn't have to try too hard to hear the two women reminiscing about the 'old days' while Gran put the kettle on. But to make sure he didn't miss anything, he crept forward to sit in the passageway with Troop and Ginger. Mostly they talked about people Sam had never heard of, but then there was a pause and he heard Libby ask, 'So what brings you back here, Mother Merryweather?'

Mother Merryweather? That was what the girl had called her.

'I got the call, Libby,' Gran said. 'Right out of the blue. It shook me something rotten, I can tell you.'

'From here?' Libby sounded shocked. 'Someone contacted you from here?'

'They surely did. And the word Dreables was mentioned.'

'Never,' said Libby, sounding shocked.

'Indeed it was. But you sound surprised, Libby. I assume that means you've seen nothing?'

'Not a thing,' Libby said.

'Of course, that doesn't mean a lot. Dreables don't usually make themselves visible to adults anyway.'

'I shall be vigilant from now on, Mother Merryweather, you can be sure of that. Now, I've just made some fresh vanilla custard tarts for the bakery and I've brought some for you. Would you care for one with your tea?'

Sam heard the sudden rattle of crockery, as if a hand holding a cup and saucer had begun to tremble uncontrollably.

'Care for one of your vanilla custard tarts?' Gran said in a trembling voice. 'Do dogs like bones?'

Sam heard plates being put onto the wooden table followed by the sound of Gran wimpering – which usually accompanied her catching sight of something delicious from the bakery world.

'Eese aah underful,' Gran said through a full mouth. 'Eely underful, mmmm...'

Suddenly, Gran was cut off in full flow, like someone turning off the switch of a radio. There followed a sudden silence and then a faint choking noise and then a very loud thud, like something heavy falling to the floor. Sam wanted to run to the kitchen door to see what was going on but he stopped himself. Every fibre in his body screamed out at him that it was something bad. There were more seconds of silence before a new noise, a horrid, low grunting noise, began to emerge from the kitchen. From within that noise emerged a chuckle and finally words – of a sort – around the chuckle. And they were not particularly pleasant words at that.

'Sleepy, sleepy tricksy…He's got you, Mother Merryweather, heh, heh, heh…Serves you right for scoffing… serves you right for scoffing the sleepy tricksy tarts. Heh, heh.'

There was more shuffling, and Sam had just enough time and sense to dash back into the bedroom before Libby appeared in the passageway. Except it wasn't the Libby he'd seen moments before. This Libby was hunched over so that her knuckles brushed the floor when she walked – in fact, it was more a shamble – towards the front door, which she proceeded to open. Then Troop growled again. Slowly, the Libby thing turned towards him.

'Horrible doggy and disgusting moggy. Want some sleepy tricksy cakes? Come on, nice doggy.' Libby retrieved a vanilla custard tart from a wicker basket in her hand and lobbed it towards Troop. It landed right in front of him. The dog sniffed it and whined, but he didn't eat it.

'Bah...horrible doggy. He'll send someone for you, he will. Make you into soup, he will, heh, heh...'

Troop growled louder and to his delight, Sam saw Libby Brown flinch. And then the most horrible and weird thing he'd ever seen in his life took place in front of his eyes. Libby Brown started to shake and shudder in front of him. Something was happening to her. A shadow appeared around her, a fuzzy shape that was accompanied by a gluey sucking noise like trying to unstick a plunger from a tile floor. Something was separating itself from Libby Brown. Something that was disgusting to look at. It was vague and somehow insubstantial, but it had a big knobbly head and a bowed over body with long arms to the ground and tusks for teeth and small, pig-like eyes. There was a final gloopy pop and Libby Brown, or the body of Libby Brown, collapsed to the ground, leaving the other phantom shape in the passageway staring at Troop and Ginger.

'Bah,' it said finally and shuffled off through the door.

Sam emerged, trembling, from his 'bedroom.' He waited until Troop went slinking to the front door and looked back with a faint wag of his tail. It was only then that Sam dared run towards the door, jumping high over Libby Brown as he did so, and slam the door shut. He sat down with his back to the closed door and hugged Troop's big head.

'I'm glad you're here, Troop,' Sam said, hearing the tremor in his own voice. He looked down as a second warm furry body rubbed against his leg. 'Okay,' said Sam, 'and you too, Ginger.' But it was hard to ignore the big lump that was Libby Brown in the passageway. Her chest was moving up and down quite faintly and he crept forward on his knees to look at her face. It was peaceful but very pale. He turned and stood up and went in to the kitchen. Gran was lying in an untidy heap under the table. She was as pale as Libby Brown but she too was breathing slowly and steadily.

'Gran,' said Sam, shaking her gently, 'Gran, wake up.'

She didn't stir.

'Gran, please. What's happened to you?' He heard the cry in his voice but was helpless to stop it. 'Gran, please wake up. Please. I don't want to be here on my own, please.'

He shook her more forcibly, but still she didn't respond. He got up and fetched some water from the tap and splashed it on her face. That worked in all the films. But it didn't this time. Stifling a sob, he stood up and saw the vanilla custard tarts on the table. Quickly, he scooped them all up and threw them in the bin under the sink. He even fetched the one from the passageway – just in case Troop was tempted – and all the while he was thinking about what he should do.

The police! Of course. That was it.

He found the phone in the living room. He picked up the receiver but it sounded odd. In fact, it sounded of nothing. There was no dialling tone. After a while, he heard some snuffling and grunting on the other end, like someone was listening. Quickly, Sam put the receiver down again. It was no good. He was stuck in the cottage with his gran and Libby Brown unconscious and there was no help from the police and it was starting to get dark outside. With heart as heavy as Gran's old iron poker and his brain full of frightened confusion, Sam went around the cottage from room to room to make sure all the windows were locked tight and the doors bolted. Then he went back to Gran and made her comfortable with a cushion and a blanket and did the same for Libby Brown.

He ran some water into a glass from the tap and took it to his bedroom with Troop and Ginger. He took the suitcase off the bed where Gran had dumped it earlier, drew the curtains and sat on the springy mattress. Sam didn't know what was happening, but he did know that something was very, very wrong with this place. Eventually he lay down with Troop next to him and Ginger standing guard in the doorway. He dozed fitfully in a dreamless sleep. Twice he woke up to the sound of Troop growling quietly. Sam held his breath to listen. Outside he could hear grunts and shuffling noises and sometimes deep chuckles. Once he heard the noise of scrabbling from the front door and he was really, really glad he'd locked and bolted it.

'I know what they are,' Sam whispered to Troop in the darkness. 'I know what they are and why Gran is here.' He reached out and touched Troop's fur and felt

Ginger rub against him and was never gladder of their company than in that dark moment.

'They're the Dreables, aren't they?'

Neither the dog nor the cat made any noise in response. But they didn't need to because deep down Sam knew he was right.

DREABLES

Sam must have fallen asleep between Troop and Ginger. When he opened his eyes, it was light outside. He went to the toilet and almost fell over Libby Brown on the way back. He checked on Gran and she seemed to be okay, but her face was the colour of his white bed sheets at home, and his efforts at waking her again were just as useless as the day before. He drank some water and realized that he was starving. Memory of the vanilla tarts in the bin made his stomach burble and he made himself forget them. He fetched a chair to stand on and looked through the cupboards. Gran had brought some tins of food with her; broccoli, tinned peaches, mulligatawny soup as well as porridge, boil in the bag rice with peas, and, to top it all, dried figs. It was as if she had made a list of all the things that Sam hated most in the world and decided to bring them with her.

He wouldn't, couldn't bring himself to eat any of that stuff.

Under the sink, Gran had stashed some dog and cat food and Sam opened a sachet of salmon and prawn in jelly for Ginger and lamb with peas and carrots for Troop. It smelled disgusting, but the look of it made Sam even more hungry than he'd been.

'I wish Gran had brought just one thing I liked,' he said as Troop and Ginger tucked in.

It was then he remembered Mrs Walpole's cherry Bakewells, and his stomach did an instant impression of a small earthquake at the very thought of them. He jumped up and ran to the front door. He slid back the bolts and pulled it open very gently. Outside, there was no sound of aeroplanes or cars or birds. The road was empty, and the garden looked quiet too. The car was exactly where Gran had parked it. But then he remembered the key. He closed the door, ran into the kitchen, and found the keys in Gran's handbag on the draining board. He opened the front door again and pressed the unlock button on the key fob. Two flashes of orange lights and the car unlocked itself.

Sam waited.

Nothing happened.

Sam took three deep breaths and sprinted for the bush he'd hidden behind when Gran had first gone into the house. He looked up and down the road – still empty. Then he made a dash for the car. The cakes were still on the passenger seat in the Tupperware box. Quickly, Sam grabbed them and ran for the house. It was only as he got to the threshold of the front door that he saw the deep claw marks gouged into the wood. They hadn't been there yesterday. Memory of the scrabbling noise he'd heard the night before sent a deep shudder through him. He stepped inside and closed the door behind him. Troop was sitting in the passageway looking stern.

'I had to, Troop,' Sam said. 'I'm starving.'

He hurried to the bedroom, sat on the bed, and opened the box of cakes. Twenty-four large cherry Bakewells sat there. Gran had obviously not been tempted on the journey down. He took one out and bit into it. An explosion of fantastic flavours detonated in his mouth. Never, in all his ten years of life, had he tasted anything better. The rich cherry jam mingled with the sweet almond extract and the crumbly pastry and Sam closed his eyes in ecstasy. He ate three right off. He drank some more water and within five minutes felt a great deal better.

'Thank you, Mrs Walpole,' he said to Troop and Ginger, who were by this time watching him patiently. 'Okay,' said Sam, nibbling his fourth cherry Bakewell, 'this is what I know. Dreables are horrible. But they don't like you two and according to Gran, adults can't see them, but I can, and I bet you can too. Somehow, they've put Gran and Libby Brown to sleep and we have to do something to help them. But this place is really spooky, and I can't phone the police. So that leaves us with just one person who can help and that's the girl that sent for Gran in the first place. Trouble is, I don't know her name or where to find her...'

Troop stood up and whined and trotted towards the back door. Ginger followed in his own cat time.

'Want to go out, boys?' Sam asked.

Troop wagged his tail, but when Sam opened the back door for him, he just stood resolutely at the door and both he and Ginger just kept looking at Sam. Neither of them moved.

'This is no time for a walk,' Sam said, but then an idea hit him between the eyes. 'Do you know where the girl is?'

Troop's tail started wagging and Ginger's shot straight up.

'That's why Gran brought you, isn't it?'

The tails did their thing.

'Okay, but we need provisions. Just wait a minute.'

He rummaged in an old boot room and came up with a dusty rucksack into which he put another half dozen cherry Bakewells, including the half-eaten one he'd nibbled, and a plastic water bottle that he washed out and then filled from the cold tap.

'Okay,' he said finally to Troop and Ginger. 'Let's go.'

SAM FOLLOWED as the cat and dog left through the back gate of the cottage. Instantly, they were out onto an open field. To their right, beyond two more fields, the open moor seemed to stretch away forever with no sign of habitation. They crossed the field and went through a gap in a dry-stone wall and Troop immediately turned in the direction of the village. But Sam could see that if he kept low, no one would see them from the roadway. On the far side of the road, less than a mile away, Sam was struck again by the regular mounds of grass-covered earth. He counted seven of them. Beyond, there were bigger hills which were topped by the white mist that still encircled the narrow vale. The morning was bright but there was a chill in the air that seemed to seep through Sam's clothes and in to his bones out here on the moor.

Troop led them for ten minutes until they reached the far end of the village. There the dog stopped. There was another gap in the stone wall and a path which led directly down to the road. From where they sat, waiting and watching, Sam looked back at a sign on the road that said,

Welcome to Wihtlea on the Barrows.

Weird name for a very weird place.

'Now what?' Sam asked Troop.

The dog whined and looked up and down the road and then swiftly trotted down and across to the other side. Ginger followed with Sam at the rear. They were quite near the houses now but still Sam saw no one.

Troop ducked behind a fence and Sam followed. The place seemed like a ghost village with none of the usual noises of children playing, or cars revving or ice-cream vans chiming that you would expect.

But then they did hear a sound. The sound of a child laughing. Troop's ears pricked up. He trotted up the road to a small park. At the far end of the park was a children's play area. To his utter amazement, a woman and a small boy were in the park, the boy laughing with delight as the woman stood behind him, pushing him higher and higher on the swing.

Hope flared in Sam's heart. An adult. That meant she would know what was going on. But then he saw the way she was glancing around, her head turning towards a car that had been parked close to the other entrance to the park. It was loaded with camping equipment and the front doors were both open. It looked like she was waiting for someone. The child was no more than four or five, squealing with delight as he went higher and higher on the swing.

Sam wondered if they'd stopped for a break on their way to somewhere else. Perhaps there was a man who had gone off for supplies or to find a toilet. It had happened to Sam on trips with his parents before now. He thought about walking over there and introducing himself. He thought about what he might say. It was going to sound really weird, but then he didn't have much choice.

But Troop wasn't moving. He wasn't even looking at

the child; he was looking off to the left, to where the strange grassy mounds began. Sam followed the dog's gaze. Something was moving, loping down from between the furthest mounds. The child on the swing saw it too and began pointing, but the woman seemed oblivious. She just carried on pushing the child. Sam could only stare in frozen horror at what happened next.

It was difficult to make out what exactly the thing was, but Sam could guess. It seemed as if the air shimmered about it and Sam thought he could hear it grunting as it ran, its long arms reaching forward to the ground like a gorilla's. It was making straight for the woman, but she seemed totally unaware, whereas the child was turning in the chair swing to watch its approach with growing alarm.

But there was no stopping the thing. It flew straight at the woman. It seemed inevitable that she would topple over but the most curious thing of all was that she didn't. The thing seemed to smash right into her, to become one with her like two bits of Plasticine thrown together. She swayed slightly and then put out her hand to slow the child's motion on the swing and quickly, she got him down.

They started walking towards the grassy mounds, the little boy holding up his hand for his mother to take. But she seemed distracted, lost in thought, and the hand remained empty. Sam stayed hidden, flitting from tree to tree around the edge of the park, keeping them in sight. But Troop wasn't moving.

'Come on,' Sam said. 'I have to see what happens'

Troop got up and followed. The park narrowed to a point under the ruin of a stone archway which led through to a group of standing stones and a line of dark gorse and brambles, beyond which sat the mounds. By the time Sam and the animals had reached the point where they could go no further except over another stone wall, they could see the standing stones quite clearly. It was here the child and its mother stood. Suddenly, the woman turned to the child and said, 'Let's play hide and seek.'

The little boy nodded vigorously.

'Me first,' said the woman. 'You go in to the middle of those stones and count to twenty. I'll hide.'

The boy immediately ran to the centre of the ring of stones and put his hands over his eyes and began counting. The woman didn't hesitate. Sam had played hide and seek in ruined castles with his dad when he was about this boy's age. He knew the rules. His mum or his dad were never far away, and they'd leave little clues to make it easy for him to find them. But this wasn't what was going on here. The woman turned and ran back through the archway as quickly as she could and turned left towards a patch of reeds and bushes. When the count got to nineteen, Sam saw her collapse onto the ground in the middle of the undergrowth. She was totally out of sight. It was as if she'd never existed.

When the boy looked up, he shouted, 'Ready or not,' and began looking about him. But there was no sign of his mother.

'Mummy,' he cried, instantly aware of the fact that this was not a version of the game he was used to playing. 'Mummy, where are you?'

But the boy's confusion was momentary, because his attention, like Sam's, was suddenly drawn to what was happening around him inside the stone circle. Out of the ground in front of each of the standing stones something was erupting. They looked for all the world like the tops of huge mushrooms, but it was soon clear that these were just the heads of something far worse than fungi. Barrel chests followed and then long, muscled arms. In seconds the circle was full of lumpy, horrid, grunting things, dribbling saliva and stretching and yawning.

'Dreables,' whispered Sam.

The little boy screamed in terror and instinctively turned to run. Too quick and nimble for the Dreables, he slipped between them and for a moment it looked as if he might break free, but at the very point of breaking through the circle, he fell backwards as if he'd run straight into a wall. Then they were upon him. One of them had a net and within ten seconds and despite his kicking and screaming, they had him in their clutches, laughing at his moans and cries for help.

Sam's instinct was to get up and go to the boy, but even as he pushed himself up from his crouched position, he found he couldn't move. Something had his trouser leg in its grasp. Sam looked back. It was Troop.

'Let go, Troop,' Sam protested. 'We've got to help him.'

But Troop had his jaws clamped on Sam's jeans and wouldn't let go. When Sam turned back to the ring of stones, it was empty. The boy and the Dreables had all gone.

Sam gave up fighting Troop and hit the ground with his fist angrily.

'I hate Dreables even more now.'

Troop whined and let go of Sam's jeans.

'Okay, I won't go after them, but I have to see if his mother is alright,' Sam said.

They found her near a stagnant pool. Sam pulled her away from the water as best he could and made her comfortable in the way he had Gran and Libby.

They left the woman and Sam followed the cat and the dog again, his mind reeling from what he had just witnessed. What the Dreables had done – using the little boy's own mother to trick him – was horrid and disgusting. More than anything, it made Sam very, very angry.

They headed back towards the village but stayed on its edge. Troop came to a stop at the bottom of what looked like a very long garden, at the end of which were four big sheds built into a bank. In front of the end shed, two big and particularly ugly-looking Dreables were snoozing in beaten-up armchairs.

Sam could see that they were different from the thing that had been in Libby Brown. These were very solid creatures of the earth, just like the things that had stolen the little boy. They were covered in lumps of mud and parts of their bodies were craggy and scabbed with lichen, as if they had been wrought of the very ground they sat on. Their snores rumbled in the still air and a very large collection of flies buzzed around their heads, resulting in the occasional flailing Dreable arm being thrown up to ward them off.

'Know what flies like more than anything, don't you, Troop?'

Troop made a low grumbling noise in his throat.

'Is that where she is? In that shed?'

Troop whined again.

'So how do we get to her? I don't fancy creeping past those things.'

Troop trotted away to the left and waited for Sam to follow. The dog took them the long way around, back through some of the streets they'd just slunk along to the opposite end of the garden. There were some big wooden gates and a sign that said; *Beety's Market Garden – home grown vegetables for sale.* This side of the garden was covered over by long tunnels of polythene. Troop went into the first and trotted along its length. The polythene was too opaque to see through and the tunnel was sealed at the far end, but this was where Troop now stood, whining softly. Sam tried, but soon realised that it was too thick to tear with his hands.

'Wait here,' Sam said and backtracked along the tunnel. He was looking for a toolbox, but he found something better. In an old wheelbarrow, on top of some mud-encrusted gloves, sat a pair of pruning shears. Sam took them and quickly poked a hole through the polythene and slit it right up the middle to make a door. There was now a ten-foot gap of open ground between them and the end shed, in full view of the Dreables. But they were snoozing. Ginger went first, then Troop, and finally Sam, the three of them sliding around the side of the end shed. But the Dreables' snores continued without interruption.

'Right,' Sam said, catching his breath. 'That was close. Still, we're here now. So, let's find the girl.'

POPPY STEVENS

They crept around to the rear of the sheds which had been built into the bank of earth behind. There wasn't much room and the ground was littered with discarded plastic sacks which had once contained chicken manure. It was a warm day. The smell was not exactly pleasant, and Sam found himself dabbing his eyes to stop them running. They eased their way along until they were just a few feet away from the snoozing Dreables. Above them, in the rear wall of the shed, was a small window. Sam found some tiny pebbles and threw them one at a time up at the grimy panes. After the fifth one struck, he heard a voice.

'Go away, you Dreables!'

It was a small girl's voice. The same one he'd heard that morning from within the cloud of mist – or whatever it was – that had erupted from Gran's car.

'Shh,' Sam said, alarmed that her voice would alert

the things in the chairs. 'We're not Dreables.'

'Yes, you are, you're horrible Dreables but you can't come in here, so go away.'

'We're not Dreables,' protested Sam an as loud a whisper as he dared. 'Look, I've got animals with me.'

He heard some movement from inside the shed and an eye appeared behind the window.

'You've got a cat and a dog? How come?'

'They're my gran's.'

'Your gran's? Who's she then?'

'My gran, that's who she is. You sent a message to her this morning, didn't you?'

'Mother Merryweather? You came with Mother Merryweather?' There was no denying the sudden excitement in the girl's voice.

'Gwladys Merryweather is my gran's name, yes. Look, I'm Sam Jones and this is Troop and Ginger.'

The window opened another inch and Sam saw two bright blue eyes staring down at him.

'How did you get past them?'

'We sneaked. They're still there, snoozing out the front. Is there another way in?'

The girl shook her head. 'I double-locked the door with onions. They don't like onions. No one can come in unless I let them.'

'Okay. What's your name?'

'Poppy. Poppy Stevens.'

'What's going on, Poppy? Who are the Dreables?'

'Wait a minute. If you are Mother Merryweather's

grandson, you'd know about Dreables.'

'No, I wouldn't. She tells me all sorts of stuff, but she's never told me about Dreables.'

Poppy seemed to hesitate and think. 'Maybe not. Mother Merryweather wouldn't speak about them unless she had to. It's bad luck. The only things that want to talk about Dreables are Dreables.'

'Well, I'm not a Dreable.'

'You don't look like a Dreable. And them animals look real. But Dreables can steal voices. That's how they get you at night. Make themselves sound like your friend so's you open the window and they grab you out of your bedroom.'

'Well, I'm not a Dreable,' insisted Sam, but his mind did a cartwheel at what Poppy was telling him. 'I'm Sam Jones.'

'Say Mother Merryweather's mantelpiece.'

'What?'

'Say it. Dreables won't say it. It makes them go all funny if they say it.'

'Mother Merryweather's mantelpiece,' Sam said, feeling a little bit awkward.

There was the sound of movement in the shed and then the window opened, and Poppy propped it up on a metal stay. Sam could see two-thirds of her face now and along with the blue eyes there were freckles and two braids of plaited hair. She was younger than Sam by a year or two, he guessed.

'You're definitely not a Dreable,' whispered Poppy,

and her face suddenly lit up. 'But if you're here and Mother Merryweather is too, it means we can fight them.'

'Whoa,' Sam said. 'Fight the Dreables?'

'Yes. Mother Merryweather knows how. She's the only one who does.'

Sam frowned. The idea of Gran fighting anyone at the best of times was pretty weird. But the Gran that he'd left passed out on the floor of her cottage was not capable of fighting anything.

'My gran hates fighting. She always tells me to be extra polite to people who want to fight you. She says it takes away their power.'

'She's a cunning lady is Mother Merryweather. That's what they all say.'

Sam wanted to tell her about Gran and Libby Brown, but somehow, he couldn't quite do it at that moment. He needed to know what was going on.

'Poppy, what exactly are Dreables?'

'They're things that used to live in the Barrows. My gran said they were here before there was telly and cars and roads and stuff. They used to do horrible things to people that got lost on the moor. My gran told me that a Wiht Warlock made them to be his army. He made them from things that lived under the ground.'

Sam made a face. 'I've never heard of them before.'

'All the children that live in Wihtlea know about them. We know not to go poking in caves and stuff. But that doesn't stop the tourists.'

'What do you mean?'

'It happened last week. Pot holers going where they shouldn't have. They found a bottle. Just an old bottle. But inside it was a piece of parchment with some writing on it. They showed it on the local TV.'

'What did it say?'

'I can't say it. You mustn't say it.'

Poppy disappeared, and Sam heard her moving about. She came back and thrust a piece of paper at him out through the window. There were letters on it in red crayon. Sam tried to read what was written:

Dynnargh a-berved ein breddwd.

'What does it mean?'

'If you read it out loud it gives them permission to come into your dreams. Stupid adults anyway. That's how it starts. Once they get in, they make you do things. It only needs one person. They made Mrs Hopkins go to the standing stones and let them all out.'

Sam was shaking his head. It all sounded completely mental.

'Where is everyone else, Poppy?'

'In the Barrows, I expect. The Dreables like to put them to sleep. That way they'll keep longer. The Dreables are hungry and they haven't eaten for a long time, maybe thousands of years, my gran said.'

'You mean they eat people?'

'Animals mostly, my gran said.' Poppy's voice fell. 'They keep the people for something else.'

Sam remembered the thing he'd seen in the cottage. 'I saw a Dreable in my grandmother's cottage. At least I think I did. And I saw one in the park. It was like it was a ghost and it just ran into a woman's body.'

'Those are the Dreable wraiths. To begin with, they can only get in through dreams. But now they're stronger they can possess adults because adults can't see them. But we can see them, and they can't possess us. They send the drones after us.'

'Those two outside, are they drones?'

Poppy nodded. 'They're lazy and smelly and solid. But they like frightening the little ones. That's what he really likes, the boss of the Dreables. He likes frightening us. It's what he feeds on.'

'That's why he takes children?'

'Yes,' Poppy said in a very small voice. 'He locks them up in the dark and tells them things. Horrible things.'

A chill wind gusted around them and in the shadow of the shed, Sam shivered. 'What about this fog, is that Dreables stuff too?'

'It's called the creeping Nule.'

Sam shook his head. 'I still don't know what my gran has to do with all of this.'

'My Granny Stevens and your Granny Merry-weather grew up together here. My gran's job was remembering and telling everyone else to mind the Dreables to make sure it never happened again.'

'In case what ever happened again?'

'This,' Poppy said. 'The Dreables getting out and stealing people and animals to eat and taking the children and locking them in dark caves and whispering horrible things to them so they'll cry and be miserable and waste away. My gran died last year, and she made me the Keeper. She told me what to do. How to call the cunning woman.'

'Gwladys Merryweather?'

Poppy nodded.

Sam swallowed. There didn't seem much choice now. Poppy ought to know. 'They tricked my gran too, Poppy. They tricked her into eating a cake and now she's gone to sleep and I can't wake her.'

Poppy stared at him. She didn't make any noise, but two very big tears started to run down her face. 'Then I don't know what else to do,' she said. 'Are you sure Mother Merryweather didn't tell you anything?'

Sam thought about all the stuff his gran had said to him and how he'd not really listened to any of it. But he was pretty sure that she hadn't ever said anything about how to fight Dreables. He didn't tell Poppy that his gran didn't even know he was here. She didn't look as if she could take much more.

'Maybe I can go for help. The Dreables don't actually know I'm here. How far is it to the next village?'

'Five miles to Lockley. But Constable Booker went yesterday, and he hasn't come back.'

'Stay here,' Sam said. 'Lock the window and don't let

anyone in. It's only five miles and I'm used to walking. That shouldn't take more than a couple of hours. I'll be back in no time.'

Poppy just blinked. There was desperation in her face. 'But she's supposed to pass it on. She's supposed to teach you what to do.'

'Well, she didn't, okay?' Sam felt his face flush angrily. This wasn't his fault. Why had Gran not told him any of this? 'Stay here,' Sam urged. 'We'll be back. Promise.'

He turned and the three of them tiptoed back to the poly tunnel and out onto the street. Troop and Ginger seemed to know what was expected of them and Sam didn't need to ask. Just as well because he was too caught up with his own thoughts. He felt confused and a little bit scared. This was really weird stuff. The sort of stuff he normally liked to read about. But being in it, an actual part of it, wasn't that much fun at all, he decided. But most of all he felt stupid. All the time his gran had been on at him for liking things like ogres and ghosts, and yet she'd grown up in a village where they had the real thing. So why hadn't she told him any of it?

An answer did pop into his head, but it wasn't one he liked very much so he got rid of it and turned his attention to the task ahead. Above him lay the hills he and Gran had driven across.

Just a little yomp, he told himself as he hurried along after Troop and Ginger.

THE CREEPING NULE

Troop led them back the way they'd come across the park to the edge of the village. It was mid-morning now, but the roiling mist still clung to the tops of the hills. Troop stopped short of the road itself and stayed on a well-worn path that ran parallel to it as it meandered up and over the moor. Sam saw a wooden marked post engraved with the sign of an acorn and knew that this was a walker's path. It climbed steadily and after a mile, Sam stopped to look back at Wihtlea on the Barrows. What he saw was a sleepy village with sandstone walled, slate-roofed houses lining winding streets. The whole landscape was quilted with patchwork gardens. But it was all eerily silent. No roar of motorbike nor bark of dog nor cry of child broke the unnatural stillness.

Sam could feel the mist against his skin now; a cold damp kiss. It grew thicker as they climbed and the temperature started to fall. Sam was already sorry that he hadn't borrowed one of Gran's old coats from the cottage. Thinking of Gran alone on the kitchen floor made Sam walk a bit faster. Troop and Ginger kept up well but neither of them strayed from the path as the mist closed in about them.

They'd gone about a mile and a half from the village when Sam realised he was having difficulty breathing. For a minute he wondered if they'd climbed the last couple of rises a bit too quickly, but they were mere bumps in the landscape compared with the coastal cliffs he'd tramped with his mother and father. Sam glanced at the animals. Troop's tongue was hanging out and Ginger didn't look all that comfortable either with his ears back and his tail down. Worse, a dreadful feeling of tiredness had suddenly come over Sam and the mist had thickened to the extent that he couldn't see more than twenty yards ahead or behind.

'Let's just rest for a minute,' Sam said.

Troop whined.

'Just for a minute,' Sam insisted. He sat on a boulder at the edge of the path. Maybe if he just lay down for a while and shut his eyes, he'd feel better. The common-sense part of his head – filled with mountaineering wisdom by his parents – knew that going to sleep on a mist-covered hill was a very, very silly thing to do. But he was just so awfully tired. Troop began making more noise, growling low in his throat, but Sam could hardly hear him. It was as if his ears and his eyes and even his mouth were being stuffed with cotton wool.

Sam's stomach rumbled. It was complaining again but he didn't feel that hungry, just tired. So very, very tired. It was no good. He would have to just shut his eyes. His stomach growled again in a prolonged and loud gurgle.

'Okay, okay,' Sam said, his eyes now barely open. 'Just shut up. One cherry Bakewell should do the trick.'

Half dazed, Sam reached into the rucksack and found the half-eaten cake from that morning which he'd wrapped in kitchen paper. It would have to do. He couldn't even smell the almonds anymore. Forcing himself to, he took a bite.

The result was astonishing. As soon as the flavours hit his mouth, a light bulb lit up the dark and miserable basement his mind had become. An electric charge erupted from his taste buds and jolted all his senses into life. The lethargy and tiredness dropped away like a musty old blanket and, for the first time since they'd entered the creeping Nule, the truth of his predicament was revealed in sickening detail.

It wasn't just a mist.

Wispy tendrils were pouring down the hillside like the tentacles of a million-armed octopus. And, like an octopus, there seemed to be a purpose. Sam watched the white fingers curling around Troop and Ginger's bodies, coiling and uncoiling. Looking down at himself, he saw that they were doing exactly the same to him. This was not a hill fog, this was a clinging, strangling, breath-stealing Thing and they'd walked straight into it.

Sam clawed at the strands around his face and nose, but like the fog it was, his fingers passed right through them with a swirl. Worse, the strands reformed immediately. Alarmed, he saw that Ginger was in real trouble now. His breath was coming in ragged gasps and he was sitting on the ground, not even trying to get up. Trying to fight off these tendrils was like trying to shovel air, but Sam knew he had to do something. He turned back the way they'd come, but the Nule had closed in like a white wall and Sam couldn't be sure anymore which was forward or back.

Suddenly, he realized his mouth was still full of cherry Bakewell. He'd been so shocked by the sight of the living Nule that he'd forgotten to swallow it. He took another chew and again the flavours exploded in his mouth. Clarity replaced mud. What would Gran do?

The thought brought with it an instant memory of Gran's car stopping in the mist on this very moor and he visualised exactly what Gran had done. He took a deep breath and blew out air as if he was trying to clear an unruly fringe from his forehead. The white tendrils writhed away like they'd been burned and instantly, Sam found he could breathe normally. He ran over to Troop and blew air all over him. The dog shook himself and immediately began to trot in a different direction from the way they'd been going. Sam grabbed Ginger and blew all over him too.

'Lead on, boy,' Sam said to Troop and grabbed the dog's furry mane with his other hand. Sam blew hard into the air in front of them, and just like had happened with Gran, the mist parted.

From high above in the hills, there came a muted roar of rage.

Something wasn't going to get a boy, a dog, and a cat for supper tonight, thought Sam with satisfaction. When the three of them were able to breathe quite easily again, Sam set Ginger down and they broke into a trot. They dropped back down the hill and when they were a half a mile from the valley floor, the mist finally gave way and Sam stopped, hands on knees, breathing hard.

'No way out,' he gasped to the animals, who both turned to look at him sadly. Troop's tongue was lolling and Ginger simply began licking his fur.

'Okay, plan B,' Sam said eventually. 'Back to Poppy and find out if we can do this another way.'

THEY BACKTRACKED, being careful to stay out of sight as much as they could. But when they got to the entrance to the market garden, there were no Dreables snoozing in the battered armchairs. Worse, the door to Poppy's shed was open. With a moan, Sam abandoned stealth and ran towards the door. Inside, it was very warm and smelled of creosote and earth. Poppy's meagre supplies were piled in one corner; a bottle of water, biscuits, some bread, and a jar of blackberry jam. Sam sat heavily on a rickety wooden chair and tried to stop the tears from coming. Troop and Ginger sniffed about, but they did so half-heartedly, their tails down as they shared in Sam's misery.

'But how did they get in? She was so sure she was safe.' He glanced at the door. A string of onions still hung there.

Sam shook his head. Despite Troop and Ginger nearby, he felt alone and a little frightened. He couldn't leave to get help and he had no idea how to help Poppy. But he couldn't stay in that shed either.

'Let's go and check on Gran,' he said to Troop wearily. The dog wagged his tail in approval.

They met no one and saw nothing on the way back to the cottage. But there was one difference from the way things had been when they'd left that morning. Directly overhead, the sun still shone down through a pale blue sky, but there was no doubt that the Nule was creeping ever lower and had reached almost the very bottom of the hills now.

'I think we made it mad,' Sam said as he glanced up. Troop and Ginger looked at him in sympathy.

At the cottage, Sam found the key and let himself in. He fed Troop and Ginger and drank some water. Then he sat on the floor next to his gran's pale and unconscious form and took her hand.

'Gran,' Sam said, 'I'm sorry.'

Her hand felt cool and lifeless.

'I'm sorry for not staying at Mrs Walpole's and for sneaking into the car and for not listening to what you said to me.'

Gwladys Merryweather slept on.

'But I'm not sorry I'm here now to look after you.'

From the other side of the kitchen, Troop wagged an approving tail.

'The thing is,' Sam added, 'everything's a mess and Poppy's been taken and I don't know what to do.'

But Gwladys Merryweather said nothing.

What made him remember her ancient mobile, Sam had no idea. He got up and found Gran's handbag on the drainer where she'd left it. He rummaged around and soon put his hand on the chunky phone. His dad had a sleek black mobile which could email and had a dozen games and did just about everything except wash the dishes. Sam's mother had a tiny silver flip phone which was almost constantly stuck to her ear. Gran's phone, on the other hand, was the size of a small shoe and had a scratched and battered grey screen with black letters. He had never seen her text on it and all she ever used it for was to phone Mrs Walpole to tell her when she was coming to help out with the cats. Sam took the phone out and switched it on. It took an age to boot up but when it eventually did and despite Sam's encouraging urgings, there was not one bar of signal showing.

'Sugar,' said Sam. 'Sugary shining Shadwell's shadow.'

Of course, he meant to say something else altogether, but he never would in Gran's presence. Really speaking, he hadn't expected it to be that easy, but a tiny little part of him had wanted to try. Sighing, he switched off the phone and put it back into Gran's handbag.

It was while he was doing that he noticed her notebook. No more than three inches tall, it was bright red and the covers were worn. Gran used it to write notes to herself. Notes like who she needed to contact about the stuck window in the kitchen or what food to buy that week.

Sam thumbed through it idly, hoping to catch a glimpse of something that might help, although having no real clue about what that something might be. There didn't seem to be anything at all about Dreables, but there was quite a bit about dry cleaning, the different prices of bags of manure from various sources, and tea bags. Worming tablets for Ginger got a mention several times until at last a big tick appeared next to WORM-AWAY £4.59 – Ellisons. Sam quickly realised that they were sort of to-do lists since most of them had dates written in the top left-hand corner of the pages. He was at the point of losing interest when he caught sight of his own name. The date on the page was 5th August – the day before he'd arrived at Gran's for his week's holidays. Gran had written:

Sam arriving.

That in itself was hardly surprising especially as it was followed with, 'buy crunchy nut flakes' and 'sardines' – though why on earth his imminent arrival had triggered a need to get sardines he would never know. Especially since Sam hated the things.

But underneath, Gran had written something that made Sam's eyes narrow in concentration.

Sam – Wihtlea?

Will he be ready yet?

Too stubborn still?

Not ready to listen?

Stubborn? Sam thought, I'm not stubborn.

But then he remembered refusing to tidy his room the day before his mum and dad had left for Peru. And he remembered refusing to go to the museum with Gran. And then there was refusing to give her a good-night kiss.

But what about listening? He was always having to listen to what adults had to say, wasn't he? That was what being ten was all about. Sam's shoulders fell. She was right. He hardly ever listened to what Gran said really. Mainly because it had always sounded so weird and unnecessary.

Maybe amidst all the silly stuff like 'Don't cross your eyes or they might stay like that,' and 'Make sure you crush the shell of your boiled egg after eating it,' she'd said something like, 'And if you ever see a Dreable, throw a Smartie at it.'

He didn't think she had, but he couldn't be sure because the truth was he had never *really* listened. And now that he was in Wihtlea, he *really* wished he *really* had.

Sam closed the notebook and put it back in Gran's handbag. He should have listened better. He should not have wanted everything to be the way he wanted it to be. Sam went to the bedroom and lay on the bed with his arm behind his head and stared at the ceiling. He let his mind wander, let his brain do a bit of thinking. After a very long time, something Gran said, one of her many throwaway rebukes, suddenly seemed much more important than it had at the time. For a while, Sam steered his thinking away from it, because when he thought about it, the consequences of behaving the way Gran wanted him to didn't seem very pleasant. In fact, it was scarily awful. But no matter how hard he tried to come up with an alternative, there didn't seem to be any other way Sam could think of to get them out of the fix they were in.

There was nothing for it. He simply had to be polite.

THE BARROWS

It was by now afternoon and Sam's mind was made up. He gave Troop a final hug and gave Ginger's head one last rub. For the hundredth time he wished he could take them with him, but he knew it would not be fair on either of them.

He gazed at them both earnestly and said, 'There's water and biscuits for you in the kitchen. Your job is to look after Gran and Libby Brown until I come back. That's your duty. Now, I have to go and do mine.'

Sam adjusted his backpack and checked his pockets one last time. Finally, without another backward glance, he walked to the front door and let himself out. Directly above him the sky was still a clear pale blue but the creeping Nule was now kissing the tops of the barrow mounds and the afternoon sun could find no way through the mist's thick canopy. Sam could feel its chill breath on his skin and he shuddered at the memory of their fateful trip into the hills that morning. He hurried along the way that Troop had led him earlier, his breathing already loud in his throat, magnified by the deathly hush that hung over Wihtlea. Every instinct told him to turn around and go back, but Sam felt that this was the only way. Doubt dragged at his feet but locking the doors and burying his head under a pillow while Gran lay unrousable under some sort of Dreable spell would not solve anything, of that he was absolutely certain. He wished he felt braver but more than anything he wished he'd listened to his grandmother.

Just because she was old and didn't like iPods and had an ancient mobile phone didn't mean that she was stupid. Nor that what she knew was completely useless, even if it sometimes felt that way. Sam had thought that the way Gran had always insisted on never crossing on the stairs was just barmy. Or the way she always got Troop to lick Sam's arm if he ever fell over and cut his knee because it made the cut 'heal quicker' was just her being a bit mad. But now that he knew she was 'Mother Merryweather' he wasn't so sure at all.

Sam trudged along the fields, crossed the road, and made his way to the edge of the park where he'd seen the little boy and his mother. This time he didn't try and hide. What was the point? Several times he became aware of shapes moving in the shadows. Hunched over shapes with long arms that loped, but whenever he looked directly at them, there was nothing there. Nothing tried to stop him as he crossed the small playground. He walked around the roundabout and tried to slow his beating heart. He tried to tell himself that it was best to just grit his teeth and do this and not think about it too much. But it was hard. Probably the hardest thing he'd ever done.

Once, a girl in his class had come back from holiday with some sort of weird flu. It meant that everyone in his class needed an injection to stop them from getting the same illness. Their teacher, Mr Mumford, explained it all and drew diagrams of viruses and told them that they'd be called out of the class four at a time. Sam remembered waiting for his turn. Mr Mumford had decided to read them a story while they all waited. It had been a story about a woman who liked tortoises, but Sam could barely remember the details and he'd found it hard to concentrate. After the inoculation, there was tea and biscuits in the canteen so no one who'd already had the injection came back to the classroom and somehow that made it worse.

What Sam did remember was the slow walk along the corridor with his other three classmates when they were finally called. One of them kept telling him and the others how 'not' scared of needles he was and kept giggling nervously. Another went very, very quiet and pale – almost as pale as Libby Brown and Gran now were. The third, Madeline Allsop, one of the few girls Sam thought he actually liked, said that she'd heard a story that once the needle from an injection had broken off in someone's arm and had travelled all the way to their heart and killed them. Sam remembered going off Madeline Allsop very quickly that afternoon. As it turned out, the needle was tiny and the way the nurse pinched the flesh of his skin together meant that he didn't actually feel the prick one little bit. Afterwards, as he dunked a biscuit into his tea, he listened to the others comparing their flu jab technique.

'I closed my eyes and squeezed them really tight until I could see stars.' Or, 'I put a pencil between my teeth and bit on it. Now I've got bits of wood in my mouth.'

But pretty soon, everyone quietened down, and Sam realised that day that the fear of something happening is often quite a lot worse than the actual thing itself.

But then the Dreables knew that very well too.

Instead of walking around the edge of the park, Sam strode right through it. It was half past three, still quite early for a summer's day, but already the light seemed to be fading as Sam walked under the stone archway and looked at the standing stones. He didn't really know what was going to happen next, but he did have a plan of sorts. He thought of Troop and Ginger waiting for him and he thought of his mother and father so very far away, oblivious of Wihtlea and the mess he was in, and realised that he would miss them all if he never saw them again. But there was nowhere to go and no one to turn to.

Then he thought of Gran again. He knew exactly what she would have said. 'Know your enemy, Sam. Know your enemy.'

When he got to the standing stones, Sam took a deep breath and said, 'Okay. Here I am. Sam Jones, Mother Merryweather's grandson. I want to speak to you, please.'

Nothing happened. Sam stood facing the stones and began to think that he'd made a big mistake. After all, he wasn't from Wihtlea. Perhaps the Dreables didn't want anything to do with him.

'Hello?' he said again.

He counted to thirty in his head and was about to turn around when he heard a noise. It was a deep rumbling, rolling noise. As if a very heavy stone was being moved somewhere beneath him. He looked up. The largest of the standing stones was beginning to tilt backwards, leaving a hole in the ground where it had stood. In the hole were some steps that led right down into the Barrow itself. It looked about as inviting as cold spaghetti hoops on toast. But then out of the hole there came a sound. In fact, it was one of Sam's favourite sounds; Christmas bells jangling rhythmically and yes – a choir somewhere deep inside the tunnel singing 'Jingle Bells'! As Sam peered down, he saw that the hole wasn't a damp chasm into the earth but a brightly lit entrance to a magical Christmas grotto. Sam stepped forward. He could see right down into it. Inside, children were playing with toys and elves dressed in green were running around giving everyone chocolate and drinks in brightly coloured cups. One of the children looked up and saw Sam peering down. She had freckles and plaited hair.

'Sam?' said Poppy Stevens, sounding pleased. She ran up the stairs towards him. 'We were wrong, Sam. We were all wrong. It's lovely in here. It's Christmas all the time.'

Sam heard the words and knew they were coming from Poppy's mouth. A part of him, the part that loved Christmas, wanted to believe her. The smell of turkey and Christmas pudding and fruitcake and mince pies drifted up. Over Poppy's shoulder, Sam could see a table groaning under the weight of an amazing banquet. Salivating madly, Sam remembered how hungry he was.

'Come on, Sam. It's fine. Really it is.'

Sam looked at Poppy. She was smiling and there were two spots of bright colour in her cheeks. But there was something wrong with her eyes. They were a little too bright, a little too smiley, and in the whole time she spoke to him, she didn't blink even once. Sam reached into his pocket for a bit of Mrs Walpole's Bakewell.

'I don't believe you,' Sam said.

Instantly, the music died, and the lights flicked off. Poppy disappeared, and Sam was left staring into the black maw. He took another step forward and flicked on his torch. There was no Christmas grotto. There was just a cold, damp tunnel with a stony floor. Instead of laughing children, the walls of the tunnel were lined with silent, glaring Dreables. Sam began to walk down.

They watched him, sniffing the air, whispering to each other as he passed them.

' – he coming in...'

' – scrawny looking...'

' – a Merryweather supposed to be...'

Sam ignored them as best he could. He kept thinking about the little boy in the park that morning and how the Dreables had used his mother to trick him. Remembering that still made him full of a cold sort of anger. Ahead of him the tunnel forked. Which way?

Sam turned the torch beam onto a particularly ugly-looking Dreable perched on a boulder. 'Which way to the king?' Sam demanded.

The Dreable laughed out loud. 'The king is it?' He got up off the boulder and shambled over to Sam and then turned to the other Dreables like it was all a big joke. 'He wants to see the king, does this one.'

Dreable laughter echoed in the tunnel.

'Want to get it over with quick, do you?' The Dreable bared its fangs at Sam.

'Which way to the king?' Sam said.

The Dreable seemed to think for a moment. Its eyes rolled up in its head and it became particularly gormless. Sam could almost see the cogs going round. Finally, the eyes rolled back down. 'He's waiting for you,' it said. 'But he wants me to show you the sights on the way.' The Dreable chuckled malevolently.

'Just take me to the king,' Sam repeated.

'Oh, I will. I will. Follow me.'

The Dreable took the left fork. As they descended, it got colder and damper and Sam was glad he'd decided to wear a sweatshirt over his T-shirt. After thirty or so steps, Sam felt the air change. He shone his torch upwards. The tunnel had given way to a huge chamber. The Dreable had stopped. In the stark light of Sam's torch, it waved its arm and smirked.

'This is where we keep the monkeys,' it said in a cackle.

Sam swung the torch beam. The walls were lined with cages three stories high with bars running from floor to roof. At first, Sam thought they were empty, but then the light reflected off a face which quickly hid itself. Sam took a step closer. There were shapes in the cages. Huddled, miserable shapes cowering in the corners. One or two risked a glimpse of the light and Sam saw instantly that they were terrified. More than that, they had hopeless expressions, beyond despair, as if seeing the torchlight was nothing more than a dread Dreable trick.

'This is the cave of misery,' said the Dreable. 'This is where we do our best work.'

'What work?' Sam asked.

'This,' the Dreable said. Without warning it launched itself at the cages with a terrifying roar. It hit the bars with a shuddering clatter, one arm reaching in for whatever it could grasp. From within the cage, Sam heard at least a dozen screams which were echoed by other voices all around him. They were high pitched, those screams. The sort of noise a terrified child made. He tried to imagine being locked away in one of these cages in the dark, waiting for that roaring noise, waiting for a grasping hand to reach in through the bars.

'Why did you do that?' Sam asked. He could feel his face burning.

'Keeps 'em quiet, it does. We don't always bellow at them like that though. Oh, no. Sometimes we just tells 'em stories in whispers about how we're going to eat their parents or their dog. Funny thing is they cry more when we tell 'em about the dog,' The Dreable cackled again. The screams, which had died to muted sobs, rose again in isolated pockets at the sound of that cackle. Sam had seen and heard enough.

'Come on, let's go,' he said.

But the Dreable didn't seem to be in any hurry. 'What's the matter? Getting a bit twitchy, are we? Looking forward to joining your little monkey friends?' The Dreable had a malicious, confident leer in its eye. 'Want me to try out me best scarifying on you?' It drew itself up onto its hind legs and began to bare its teeth.

'Mantelpiece,' said Sam.

Instantly, the Dreable fell back onto its haunches with its knuckles on the floor. The leer had become a look of surprised confusion. 'What did you say that for?'

'Say what?'

'Mantel – ahhh.' The Dreable clamped one hand over its mouth and the other over an ear.

'What's wrong with saying mantelpiece? Is it because I'm a Merryweather?' Sam asked.

The Dreable was shaking its head, now with both its hands over its ears. It was rocking back and forth looking very unhappy. 'Shan't. Won't.'

'Right. Let's go then,' Sam said. 'And no more scarifying, thank you.'

Still with its hands over its sticking-out ears, the Dreable led on, mumbling to itself. Every few steps, it turned to look back at Sam, its eyes full of mistrust. They walked out of the cavern and back into the tunnel. Sam saw no more Dreables lounging against the walls. But there were people. The first one Sam saw was a man, leaning with his head against the tunnel, eyes shut, fast asleep. Pretty soon there were others. Sam tried to wake a couple, but it was no good. They were like Gran, frozen somehow by the Dreables, ready for whatever they wanted to do with them at some later date.

Sam lost track of time. The darkness was all about him, the walls featureless, the Dreable trudging on ahead. At last, after what seemed like hours, Sam could feel that the floor was rising and ahead he could just make out the faintest of flickering lights and guessed that it was the flame of a lit torch. The Dreable stopped and stood aside. Sam saw that the evil look was back in its eye.

'The king's waitin' for you,' it said and grinned.

It was light enough to see now and Sam flicked off his torch and walked into another huge cavern. Once inside, Sam saw that it was more like a vast hall. Huge elaborately carved pillars of stone lined the way. Statues of strange and horrible creatures stood guard in the shadows where the light faded. At the end of the hall sat a figure on a massive throne flanked by two more flickering torches. Sam walked forward. The figure shifted on the seat. It was vaguely human in shape, but Sam couldn't be sure if it was a Dreable or not. Two yellow eyes stared out at him from a hooded face. Suddenly, it spoke.

'What human dares demand an audience with me?'

Sam stopped. The voice was ancient. Older even than Gran's mobile. It sounded like the creaking open of a rotten coffin lid. The flames in the torches flickered and died down to a candle glimmer. Sam looked around him and swallowed loudly. Not for the first time since leaving the cottage, he began to wonder if he'd really made a terrible mistake.

ARGLWD

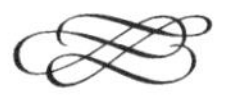

'Me,' Sam said. 'Sam Jones. It's me that wants to see you.'

'Are you frightened?' asked the king. And he asked it in a soft voice which somehow made it much, much worse.

'A bit,' Sam said truthfully.

The king bared his long, yellowed teeth. Sam thought he might have been smiling.

'Yes,' he said. 'I can taste it. Sweet and fresh.'

Sam stepped forward and flicked on his torch. The king flinched. And though Sam had seen enough to make him want to flick off the torch immediately, he kept it on. What was revealed in that harsh light was a face. At least, it might have been a face once. What flesh there was looked almost transparent, only loosely attached to the skull beneath. Within that long face were deep and hooded eyes, framed by the ragged black material of a hooded cloak. But the material, as with the flesh of its face, looked decrepit and rotten, like something that had been left out in the rain and wind for too long. Sam saw the long thin fingers of the king's hand grasp the bulbous end of the throne's armrest as he turned his head away from the torch beam.

'What have you done to my grandmother?' Sam demanded.

The light in Sam's torch died even though he hadn't touched the switch and the oily flames on either side of the throne roared and the yellow eyes flared. A wheezing noise like a cracked bellows came from the king. After a long while, he spoke.

'Not many dare enter this hall without cowering. None dare shine a light on that which has not seen day for eons.'

'What about my gran?' Sam asked again.

'The cunning woman sleeps. My faithful pets have grown cunning too. This time, her kind will not interfere.'

'What do you mean, this time?'

The yellow eyes glittered, and Sam felt an icy finger trace a line down his spine.

'What I crave is what all things crave. To live. To exist. To kill. To hunt. To taste blood as I did in the beginning.'

'What are you?' Sam asked.

'I have many names. My pets like to call me Arglwd, for I am their lord and master.'

'Stealing the children and the animals and changing the adults into your pets, that isn't right.'

Arglwd regarded Sam and tilted his head as if he was some strange curiosity. 'And yet it is my right, for I can. The cunning woman grows old and greedy. She will not stop me this time.'

He didn't know why he said it but he did. 'Then I will.'

Arglwd considered Sam and smiled. 'The brave ones taste all the sweeter when they break down and simper and wail. I will feed on your misery before morning, Sam Jones. Do not think you can hide your weakness.'

An image suddenly appeared in Sam's head. He saw his mother and father high on a mountain, walking along, enjoying the bright, sunny day. But even as Sam watched, smoky tentacles of a creeping Nule began to roll down the mountain from above. In seconds it had engulfed them and instantly, their healthy walk was a fog bound, groping struggle against the elements. The path was narrow and the mountain steep. Helpless, Sam watched as they groped forward blindly to a ledge, where they sat, clutching each other as the Nule writhed about them.

Sam shook his head and the image cleared. It was like the dream he'd had at Gran's house.

'You see,' said Arglwd. 'Your nightmares speak to me.'

'You don't know where they are,' Sam said.

Arglwd laughed. It was a very unpleasant sound. 'Enough of this pathetic bluster. You are a child and I am the ruler of this kingdom. Time now for you to suffer your fate. When we meet again, I will feed on your terror and hopelessness and misery.'

Two of the statues creaked into life behind Sam. They emerged from the shadows and Sam saw that they were huge Dreables, twice the size of the one that had brought him to the king's hall. There was something different about their eyes though. Where there should have been lustre and sparkle reflecting the light of the torches, there was nothing but a dull dead white. Shocked, Sam realised that they were blind. They prodded him with long fingers topped with pointed filthy fingernails and he could do nothing but retreat. Outside the chamber, the other Dreable waited, looking sullen.

'You didn't please him,' he moaned. 'Now we'll all suffer,' and then he added in a low whisper, 'but you will suffer the most.'

The smaller Dreable grabbed at Sam's arm and yanked at it, while the two blind dreables shuffled back into the hall. Sam half stumbled forward. They were going back the way they'd come. Back to the cages and the dark and once again Sam's head filled with the image of his parents on the mountain in the dense fog. Cold, lost, stumbling on the high path.

'Stop,' Sam ordered. 'I want to ask you something.'

The Dreable hesitated and turned back. 'Are we going to start to cry now?'

'No. I want to ask you what's it like being a Dreable?'

The Dreable stared at Sam. It was clear that no one had ever asked it that before. 'It's like bein' hungry all the time, an' waitin' to be told what to do an' enjoyin' the dark. That's what it's like.'

Sam nodded. 'I expect looking after all those terrified children is hard work.'

'You don't know the half of it. Scarifyin' isn't easy. You've got to work at it.'

'Don't suppose you ever get a thank you, do you? From the king I mean.'

'The king don't need to say thank you. He's in charge.' The Dreable eyed Sam suspiciously.

'I suppose it isn't easy to get noticed by him, being a drone.'

The Dreable exhaled loudly and shook its head. 'This place would fall flat on its bum if it wasn't for us.'

'Be nice if you could do something special for him, the king, wouldn't it?'

'Special? What you talking about?'

'What if I could help you make Arglwd feel better?'

The Dreable frowned. 'What could you have that the king wants?'

Sam rummaged in his pocket and came up with the old coin he'd found in the boxroom in Gran's house. 'Here,' he said, holding it out. 'Give him this.'

'What is it?' The Dreable stared suspiciously at Sam's outstretched hand. There was still light from the flickering torches in this tunnel and the coin glittered feebly.

'Payment,' Sam said. 'Payment from me and my gran for what he's done for us.'

The Dreable frowned again and the thick lumps on its forehead turned into mini Himalayas. 'Payment?'

'Yeah,' Sam said. 'I bet he never gets paid. Like you. Never even a thank you for all the people he steals.'

The Dreable's eyes were darting everywhere, thinking through this new little twist. 'Maybe he would like payment.'

'Be like giving him a present,' Sam said. 'A present for Arglwd from me. Only you'd get all the thanks because you brought it to him. Go on, give it to him now.' Sam held up the coin. 'Look, it even has a hole in it so he can hang it around his neck like a medal.'

The Dreable's small eyes were alight with excitement, but doubt clouded them momentarily. 'I'm supposed to put you in a cage.'

'I'm not going anywhere, am I?'

'No, you're not,' giggled the Dreable. He snatched the coin from Sam's outstretched hand and clenched it tightly in his fist. The Dreable gurgled something and two of its companions appeared out of the dark. They sat and looked at Sam while the other ran off, chattering to itself as it went. Sam waited. There really was nothing else to do. He waited and hoped, because hope was all he had.

As he'd lain on his bed in Gran's cottage thinking about duty, he'd thought of the man with the aubergine face roaring past in his car as Gran tootled along at twenty-nine miles an hour. He'd remembered how that man had waved his fist and of the way Gran had smiled and waved and the sudden change in the man's expression. The way the anger dropped away to leave shock and shamefulness.

Seconds – long, dark, and damp – ticked by. Somewhere, deep under the earth, Sam could hear the whispering rush of a river far below him. The darkness was a solid wall in front of his eyes. Only the slow, steady breathing of the Dreables gave any clue that there was another living thing in the Barrows. And Sam wondered if indeed these were living things because Arglwd hadn't looked alive. He looked like a spectre. Something that wanted to be alive but wasn't – at least not yet.

The roar, when it came, made Sam jump into the air. It was a terrifying sound, like a wounded animal. It echoed along the tunnels and reverberated off the walls so that it seemed to last for a very long time.

But deep down, Sam knew what that roar meant. It was the same noise that the aubergine-faced man would have made in his car at the sight of Gran grinning at him innocently.

Sam flicked on his torch. The Dreables watching him looked startled. Obviously the sound had troubled them too. They looked as if they weren't sure what to do, but then they saw Sam's torch and decided that perhaps making sure he remained captive was probably a good idea. They shambled forward, but their outstretched wicked nails never reached him because the air around

Sam was whirling and spinning. Above him, cracks were appearing in the roof of the cave – jagged openings that showered dust and debris but which continued to groan and rumble apart. Shafts of watery daylight pierced the darkness. It felt to Sam as if he was standing on solid ground, but when he glanced down there was nothing beneath him but the blackness of the Barrows.

It was over almost as soon as it started. With a final spurt of acceleration, Sam shot up and out into late afternoon daylight and promptly fell flat on his face onto the grass. He shook dust from his hair and sat up. He was sitting on the very top of one of the biggest of the Barrows. The crack in the earth that had ejected him rumbled again and closed, leaving nothing but a faint scar in the grass. Sam stood up. Although the Nule was above him, it had not yet reached the ground. From here he could see the whole of Wihtlea. Sam made a fist and held it up to the sky and yelled, 'Yesss!' before running down the slope, back towards the village and Gran's cottage.

Sam ran like he had never run before. He wasn't sure exactly what had just happened, but he sensed that somehow, he'd beaten Arglwd – for a while at least. As he crested the rise that led to the rear of the cottage, he saw immediately that the back door was open. He came to a full stop and his heart lurched. Suddenly, triumph turned to despair again. Troop and Ginger couldn't have opened the door. Had his little game with the Dreables annoyed Arglwd so much that he'd sent a detachment to do something horrible to the animals and Gran? He ran on, this time with fear spurring him. But as he leaped through the gap in the stone wall that led into the garden, who was coming to meet him with his tail wagging furiously but Troop himself. An instant later, Ginger appeared on top of the wall, his tail up, purring. Sam grabbed Troop and hugged him to his chest.

'Troop! Am I glad to see you. But how did you get out?'

'I reckoned they needed some air,' said a voice from the doorway.

'Gran,' yelled Sam. He was on his feet in an instant. He sprinted across the back yard and almost bowled his grandmother over as he grasped her in a hug.

'Well, this is a welcome change,' Gran said, yet she was squeezing him as hard as he was squeezing her.

But Sam didn't want to look up at her yet. He had something he wanted to say, and it seemed easier to say it into her warm shoulder. 'I'm really glad you're alright, Gran. I'm really sorry. I didn't know…I wasn't sure if what I'd done to Arglwd would…'

'Whoa, horsey,' Gran said. 'One thing at a time. Let's go inside. I've got the kettle on. Sounds like you've got a story to tell and I don't think I've ever seen anyone more in need of a cup of tea and a cherry Bakewell.'

Sam looked up at his grandmother's face and nodded.

Two minutes later he was sitting at the kitchen table drinking from a steaming mug of tea and enjoying the jam and almondy taste of the Bakewell as he poured out his story to a patient but grim-faced Gwladys Merryweather. When he'd finally finished explaining how he'd sneaked into the car because he was worried about her and ended with being ejected from the Barrows, Gran leaned back from the table and held him in her piercing gaze. But it wasn't in the disapproving way she usually looked at him when he was being stubborn or sulking; this was a totally new way. Sam wasn't sure what it was, but he'd never seen it in her eyes before.

'Well, well, Sam Jones. Aren't you the duskiest of dark horses. It looks like I got you completely wrong.'

But even though there wasn't a Samuel to be heard, Sam was expecting a telling off and he took Gran's words the wrong way.

'Sorry,' he said, letting his chin drop. 'I'm sorry I didn't listen. I'm sorry I hid in the car and…and I'm really sorry I didn't give you a kiss goodnight.'

Gwladys Merryweather leaned across the table, smiled, and kissed her grandson on the forehead.

'There. No sooner said than mended. As for all the rest, sorrow is for something you regret, not for something you should be proud of.'

Sam looked up, confused. 'But…'

'But nothing. You're my grandson and you've proved it today. Oh, I had my doubts, but not anymore.'

'But…'

'Sam, I thought I'd never get you to listen to me but obviously you have. You've looked anger and hate in the eye and been polite to both. You *paid* the king of the Dreables for what he'd done to me and was going to do to you. That was very brave of you. That's a very, *very* powerful counter curse. So powerful, it's undone everything he did to me. Congratulations.'

Gran held out her hand. Numbly, Sam took it and shook it. He knew he had his mouth open, but he couldn't help it. He was trying to work out if he'd heard correctly.

'Did you just say curse?'

'I did indeed.'

Sam shaped his mouth into another objection, but Gran held up her finger. 'What did Poppy Stevens tell you about me?'

'She said you were the cunning woman.'

Gran smiled a little smile and took another nibble at another cherry Bakewell. 'Mmmm,' she said in ecstasy, 'we'll have to send Mrs Walpole a thank you card. These are totally delicious.'

Sam frowned. 'Yeah, and that's another thing. How come I feel so much better when I eat one of Mrs Walpole's cakes? Does she use a special Mrs Walpole spice too?'

'That's for her to know and for you to find out,' Gran said, as Sam knew she would. 'But they make you feel good because they're made with love and skill, Sam. That counts for an awful lot in this world and counts for an awful lot more here and now when falsehood and despair rear their ugly heads.' Gran took another sip of her tea, but her eyes never left Sam's as she peered at him over the rim of her cup. She seemed to make up her mind as she put the cup down. 'I suppose you're going to have to know sooner or later and since you've already been to see them in their dark holes, it had better be sooner...'

'Know what?' Sam asked.

'First, have another bite of Bakewell. What I have to tell you is better heard with your mouth full of goodness. The king of the Dreables is a Wiht. It's pronounced wight but there is no g in it. He's older than a lot of those mounds he lives under. A long time ago, before books and TV and football, the world was a very different place. Things lived on the land and some under it. Old, old things. But then we came along and even though we didn't know the lore and the old ways, we were quick and cunning. Eventually, most of the old things were driven away. But in some corners of the world, they held on and dug in and used their power and the old ways to protect themselves. Some hibernated and waited for a day when we perhaps would not be so vigilant. When they could come and try again to put us in our place. Wihtlea is a place where one of the old ones hung on.'

Sam was frowning.

'Oh, you won't find it written down anywhere, but the people who live here know. And they made sure that someone always remembered the old stories about the things that lived under the ground that got into your dreams and stole the children and fed off their terror. Tabatha Stevens, Poppy's grandmother, was a Keeper. It was her job to keep the story alive.'

'But what's a cunning woman?'

Gran gave him a remorseful smile. 'Good question. I've been asking myself that ever since I woke up.' She clicked her tongue. 'Imagine letting Libby Brown's custard tart fool me.' She shook her head. 'I'm growing into an old fool. Soft and silly and forgetful.'

'But what does it mean, a cunning woman?'

'It means that we're the ones people turn to when bad things happen. We're the ones that sort things out.'

Sam pondered this. 'You mean like a witch?'

Gwladys Merryweather wrinkled her nose. 'Different breed. Bit too fond of dressing up and pointy hats and all that paraphernalia if you ask me.'

Sam's head was full of all sorts of questions, but the one that popped up first was, 'But why didn't you tell me all of this before?'

'Would you have believed me, Samuel?'

Sam hesitated. He wanted to say, yes of course, but deep down he knew he would not have. He would have thought she was nothing but a batty old fruit cake.

'No,' he said.

'That's what I like. Honesty.' Gran smiled.

'Does Mum know all this?'

'She knows about Dreables. But she thinks they're just stories.'

'Is she a cunning woman?'

Gran shook her head. 'We skip generations, Sam. It's your turn to be one of the cunning folk, not your mother's.'

'So, what now?' asked Sam.

'Now we finish our tea and then we get on with the job we came here to do.'

'And what's that?'

'Make some cakes. At least that's what we'll start with.'

'Cakes?' Sam repeated

Gran gathered up the cups and plates. From her bedroom, she retrieved her battered suitcase and put it on the table. She undid the latches and took out two pieces of ancient-looking parchment, which she put into her handbag before closing the suitcase again.

'Right, you get the eggs and I'll weigh out the flour,' she said when that was done. She adjusted one wing of her seagull glasses and from the set of her mouth, Sam knew it was pointless asking her anything else at that moment.

THE PLAN

It wasn't a difficult recipe. There was some butter and sugar, some eggs and plain flour, and baking soda, raisins, and chocolate chips. Sam had watched Gran make her amazing cookies before but this time there was one additional ingredient which Gran made up from a mixture of herbs and dried flowers that were stored in a variety of glass-stoppered bottles in a cupboard in the kitchen. The bottles had interesting-looking symbols written on the sides and Gran consulted her notebook more than once as she carefully sprinkled in the mixture. She boiled them up in a saucepan on the stove and added thirty carefully counted drops to the cookie dough mix.

They ended up with a hundred in all, which Gran put in the oven before setting the timer.

'Your basic cookie with a special Mother Merryweather twist,' said Gran, wiping her sugary hands on her apron.

'Are these for the Dreables?'

Gran gave a huge roaring laugh and dislodged one wing of her specs in the process, the immediate adjustment of which left a flour thumbprint on the glass as evidence. 'Not as long as my name is Gwladys Merryweather. No, Sam,' she added, and there was grim determination in her tone, 'these are for the children. Now, are you ready?'

'For what?'

'For a spot of clearing up.'

Sam's face fell. The kitchen was a mess. There was flour and bits of eggshell and baking powder scattered all over the surfaces.

'I don't mean here in the kitchen, Sam,' Gran explained with a frown.

'Oh,' Sam said, relieved.

'Put something warm on,' Gran ordered. 'I've just got to get a couple more things from my suitcase.'

'I suppose those are the things from the cupboard that need to be looked at because now is the time for them to be looked at,' Sam said.

Gran looked at him with an admiring smile. 'You're spot on, Sam. Spot on.'

Five minutes later, the dinger went on the oven timer. The smell of the cookies was amazing, but Gran scooped them all into a plastic bag and put them in Sam's rucksack.

'Troop, Ginger, come on, we've got work to do.' Gran grabbed her handbag and went to the cupboard under the sink and took out an old sack stuffed with half a dozen more of the same.

'What's that for?'

'For Dreables,' Gran said, and even though Sam's forehead wrinkled, she would not be drawn.

There was no sneaking out of the back this time. Mother Merryweather, Sam, Troop, and Ginger left smartly by the front door.

Outside, Sam looked around nervously. 'What if we see some Dreables?'

It was almost seven o'clock now. Still light, but the Nule was crowning the tops of the Barrows and there was an unnatural stillness in the air.

'Not if, *when* we see Dreables,' she corrected him. '*When* we do, we sort them out.'

'But how?' asked Sam. 'They're big and strong and have tusks and...'

'Are as stupid as those wooden posts either side of the gate.' Gran was positively marching down the road now, eyes peeled for any movements.

'But if they were people once don't you feel a bit sorry for them?'

'All traces of the people they might once have been have long gone, Sam. Arglwd has them exist only to feel our misery. I have no sympathy for that.'

All trace of the slight limp she usually had was gone. This was not the Gran that his mother was worried about. This was a strong and purposeful Mother Merryweather, who talked as she walked.

'We Merryweathers are who we are because sometime in the dim and distant past,' Gran added, 'a Merryweather stood up to this lot and found a way to beat them. It's in me, Sam. In you too. All we have to do is look them in the eye and say 'Bos Karrek.' It's a special curse laid on them and their kind by the first Merryweather who took them on.'

'Was she a witch?'

'No, but she did happen to be apprenticed to a nice man called Merlin.'

Sam was quiet for half a minute. Then he asked, 'What does Bosh Carrick mean? And what if they don't look you in the eye?'

'That's where their stupidity comes into it. You've already met them. There is nothing a Dreable likes more than to put on that stupid face they call 'scarifying' and bare their teeth. Once they do that, all you have to do is say Bos Karrek and they'll turn back into the lumps of rock they really are.'

'Bosh Carrick?'

'Bos Karrek. It's an incantation. It means 'Be stone.' It's old and has its origins in Welsh and Cornish, languages spoken before the Romans came and long before we started to speak English. But it has to be said by one of us. Don't ask why. Like I said, it's in us. Some special mix of voice and tone and gristle and blood and grit.'

'I don't understand.'

'No, it is a lot to take in. I remember when my gran told me, I wouldn't believe her. But there it is. Magic, if there is such a thing, is a bit like that. It's individual, otherwise everyone would be doing it and the world would be in a right pickle. Even more of a pickle that it is now. Oh, some of it can be taught, but there has to be something in you, that's all there is to it.'

'And you're sure I have it in me?' Sam asked.

Gran glanced down at him and Sam saw again that look of pride. 'Judging by what you've already done today, I'd say definitely yes. But there is only one way to find out.'

'Bos Karrek,' said Sam, trying to get it right. 'Bos Karrek, Bos Karrek. But what about Arglwd?'

'I'll deal with him when the time comes,' Gran said grimly.

THE SKWARNOK ARYON

They met the first lot on Coronation Road. A gang of them had cornered a terrified cat and were taunting it. The cat had its hackles up and seemed to be giving as good as it got. But it made Sam's blood boil to see them tormenting a small animal like that. He wanted to shout at them, but Gran put her arm out to stop him as he stepped forward.

'Don't say anything,' she said out of the corner of her mouth.

One of the Dreables saw them and immediately stood up and signalled to the others.

'Hey boys, look here. Four softies. Leave the mog, let's scarify them up for the party.'

'Oh yeah,' sang a much smaller Dreable. 'Mustn't forget the party. We always have a party for the old ones. A welcome to the Barrows party.'

'Oh please,' whimpered Gran. 'Please. Leave us alone.'

She sounded so frail and terrified that Sam had to look at her twice.

'Gran?' he asked, suddenly unsure of himself and her.

'I'd forgotten how horrible they are,' Gran said, holding her hand up in front of her eyes fearfully.

She had all the Dreables' attention now. They were leering and swaggering, enjoying Gran's terror.

'She'll be good for scarifyin',' said another of the Dreables.

'She's scarified already,' chortled another, raising itself up on its bandy back legs and pulling its long arms up over its head. It made its hands into claws and bared its teeth. Slowly it began to creep forward.

Gran, who was still cowering, suddenly dropped her hand to show her face. There was no fear there anymore. Far from it. 'Nice knowing you boys,' she said and added in a loud and clear voice, 'Bos Karrek!'

The Dreables froze, half in fear and half because they literally had frozen. They became statues. There was a sound like ice cracking on a deep lake and then the Dreables just collapsed in midair and fell to the ground as tiny pebbles, each the size of a sparrow's egg.

'Wow,' said Sam, staring at the four pebbles on the floor. 'That was… amazing!'

'It's just a question of knowing what to do and how to do it,' Gran said, scooping up the pebbles into her sack. 'Now…'

Gran didn't have time to finish her sentence. From behind her another Dreable emerged from where it had been hiding. Gran didn't see it because she had her back to it. Too late she saw the surprise in Sam's face. Before she could react, the thing was upon her, wrapping its big hands around her mouth and her waist. Troop growled and lunged forward, but the Dreable kicked out at the dog and tightened its grip on Gran.

'Call it off or I'll strangle her here and now,' it commanded.

Sam beckoned to Troop. 'Here, Troop. Here, boy.'

The dog came back to Sam and sat, growling low in its throat.

'Meddling Merryweather,' said the Dreable with its teeth clenched. 'But I've shut her up now, haven't I?' It looked terribly pleased with itself.

'Leave her alone,' Sam said. He didn't like the funny dark red colour Gran's face was becoming.

'Or what, eh, Mr sofite? If I strangles her here and now, what are you going to do about it?'

Sam watched in horror. He didn't know what best to do. Gran was the cunning woman, not him.

'Pah,' spat the Dreable. 'You wait where you are, little boy. I'll send someone back for you.' It began walking backwards, dragging Gran with it. The thing had its eyes on Troop, making sure the dog didn't spring at it.

'Wait,' Sam said.

But the Dreable wouldn't lift its eyes up from Troop. 'Too late, little boy. I'm in charge now, so just shut your softie m...'

'Please,' Sam said, taking his lead from Gran, although he didn't have to try too hard to sound as if he was pleading. It did the trick. If there was one thing Dreables loved other than scaryfying it was to gloat. Smirking, the Dreable lifted its eyes to enjoy Sam's discomfort. That glance was enough.

'Bos Karrek,' Sam yelled.

One second, Gran was in the Dreable's clutches, in another, she was just standing there, gasping for air, with a small pebble rolling around at her feet.

'Phew,' Gran said after a second of gulping in oxygen. 'That was close.'

Sam just stared at her. After a long few seconds he remembered to blink. He could feel moisture in his eyes. Gran saw it too.

'Hey,' she said and grabbed him in a hug.

'I didn't know what to...' murmured Sam.

'But you did it anyway,' Gran said. Sam looked up into his gran's twinkling eyes. She was smiling. 'That was a narrow shave. But here we are, safe and sound. There's no doubt about it now. You're a Dreable hunter too, Sam Jones. Now, just pick up that miserable specimen you just reduced to a lump of granite and pop him in the sack. We have to get on and find the Skwarnok Aryon.'

Sam picked up the Dreable. It felt warm in his hand. He wanted to ask what on earth the Skwarnok Aryon might be, but when he looked up Gran was already striding away through a gap between the houses that led up onto the open moor. He had to run to catch up with her.

'Gra-an,' Sam protested.

'It means 'silver hare,'' Gran said, not slowing down.

'Why do we want a silver hare?' Sam demanded, almost stepping in a pool of black peaty mud. They were striding up the side of a hill, and over his shoulder across the valley Sam could see the hunched Barrows, like the bent backs of huge green beasts.

'Because we need its help,' Gran said. 'The Dreables aren't the only things that lie waiting under these hills. Our ancestors weren't stupid. When a plague strikes, and half the village is struck down, if you find a herb that helps you, make sure you plant lots of it for the next time.'

Sam wanted to ask her if the plague had really struck Wihtlea but he didn't because at that moment they crested a rise. Below was a steep-sided valley at the very bottom of which ran a meandering stream bordered by a wood.

'Now,' Gran said, scanning the valley floor. 'If I remember correctly there should be a big boulder…'

Sam saw it and pointed. Gran set off immediately but when they were within fifty yards, she turned to Troop and Ginger. 'You two stay here. We don't want her frightened by two carnivores like you.'

Troop, whose tongue was lolling, tilted his head but sat where he was told to. Ginger just stood there watching.

Sam was about to ask why but then Gran was moving again. When she got to the boulder, she put down the Dreable bag. From her handbag, she took out a piece of oval amber on a leather necklace and held it up for Sam to see. It looked like there was a strand of heather caught in the middle of it. She put it over her head and knelt with one hand on the ground and the other on the boulder. She put one finger on her lips and looked at Sam and then she began to sing.

Sam realised that he'd never heard Gran sing properly, apart from lullabies when he was little. The song was strange, the words odd, but her voice was clear and pure and in the stillness of the valley, it sounded like the voice of a young girl.

Evening creeps,
The enemy is near,
Darkness roams the land.
Though friend may fall
And others fear,
Strong heart must guide our hand.
Once more we must do battle
Relive the horrors past,
And call upon our allies
Old fealties that last.
Skwarnok aryon, Skwarnok aryon
Doas yma unawath eto
Skwarnok aryon, Skwarnok aryon,
Addaw nest y gofio.

The notes trilled and soared into the air like a bird freed from a cage. Sam felt something beneath his feet, a noise or vibration that seemed to grow with every second. It came and went, as if something was moving in a circle under the ground, moving quicker and quicker until, at last, it stopped. A scrabbling, digging noise began beneath the boulder and suddenly, to Sam's utter astonishment, a head popped up from out of the grassy earth. It was a hare, but not like any Sam had ever seen. This one had a silver coat that shimmered and eyes that glittered like diamonds. She pushed herself free of the ground and sat, preening herself.

'Ah,' Gran said, like she would when a favourite song came on the radio. 'Thank you, Skwarnok Aryon.'

The hare stopped preening and bowed its head.

'Feed now,' Gran said. 'We will summon you before sunset.'

The hare hopped off towards the edge of the wood. But as it did, it seemed to leave a bright image of itself in the air wherever it went – a blurred moving silver image that faded slowly on the grass and in the air above.

'Was that…'

'The Skwarnok Aryon. The Silver Hare. She is beautiful, isn't she?'

'Yes,' Sam agreed. 'But…'

Gran was already turning away. 'Still no time for buts, Sam. We have to make use of what daylight there is left to us. Fighting Dreables at night is not any fun at all,' Gran added grimly.

She walked even more quickly on the way back to the village, picking up an excited Troop and Ginger on the way. They met no more Dreables on the way. In the park, Gran insisted on laying out the cookies they'd baked on a picnic table. But soon Sam found himself passing beneath the arch and inside the stone circle once again. Gran took Sam's hand.

'When we ask to be let in, they'll try and trick us. They'll show us something we really want, but you know it's just a sham, don't you, Sam?'

Sam remembered the Christmas party and nodded solemnly.

'I want you to put these on,' Gran said. She reached into her handbag and took out some very odd-looking pale blue gloves. They were made of fine silk and each one had an embroidered eye at the end of each finger.

'What are these?' Sam asked.

'Bislyged. When we get inside, hold them out in front of you. There are ten eyes here. The Bos Karrek will work just as well if the Dreables look at these eyes and not yours. Think of them as machine gun gloves.'

Sam could understand machine gun gloves alright. He slipped them on. They were a bit big, but they'd do.

'Ready?' Gran asked

Sam nodded, but his mouth was dry and his stomach churned.

Gran squeezed his hand and turned towards the biggest stone.

'Let us in. We are weary travellers that seek shelter. Let us in.'

'What about spells and stuff?' Sam whispered, sounding a bit disappointed.

'Like I said. Thick as two short planks, Dreables. We don't need any fancy stuff here.'

Before she'd quite finished, the standing stone started to tilt. Once again music started to drift up from below. Sam looked down to see three of his best friends from school, including Brett Hanson, sitting at the controls of the biggest video screen he had ever seen in his life. They were playing Beatty's World of Sports, which was Sam's favourite game of all time. Brett looked up at him. His face was shining with excitement.

'Sam, you badger. Where've you been? We're on level four and we need someone who can beat the pants off the Waterspector. Get down here, now.'

Sam knew how to beat the Waterspector. For just one tiny instant he felt like running down and showing them all how useless they were, but then he felt someone squeeze his hand and instantly the image faded into blackness. The only thing under the leaning stone was a black hole from which oozed an old smell of decay.

'If you go down when they ask you, there's nothing anyone can do for you. If we go down of our own accord, we stay in control.'

Sam nodded. 'It's still very dark in there, though,' he said.

'That's why we need light,' Gran said. From her bag she took a carved wooden whistle and blew on it. Sam couldn't hear anything, but Troop whined and Ginger's ears went flat. There was a noise from behind them and Sam turned to look. A silver streak appeared on the hill they'd climbed not ten minutes before. Twenty seconds later, that streak was rushing towards them across the park.

'Ready, Sam?' asked Gran.

'Ready,' said Sam.

The Skwarnok Aryon ran right past them and down into the darkness of the Burrows, leaving a dazzling silver light in its wake. Gran immediately began to walk down while Sam hesitated. But Gran didn't wait for him.

'There's cunning work to be done,' was all she said.

He didn't need telling twice. He adjusted the Bislyged and followed his grandmother down into Arglwd's lair.

THE CUNNING WOMAN

The tunnels looked very different in the Skwarnok Aryon's light and there was nowhere for the Dreables to hide. Gran went first with Sam behind and Troop and Ginger between them. Everywhere they went, Dreables dropped like flies. Gran walked like a woman in a dream with her hands out, fingers extended, and Sam could hear the hum of her voice as she repeated 'Bos Karrek' over and over.

Sam picked up the pebbles and put them in the sack. Soon, it was too heavy to carry and Gran furnished him with a fresh one. They came to a fork and suddenly Dreables started rushing at them from behind. But Sam was ready. He turned and held out his fingers and said the words in his head. The Dreables didn't stand a chance. By the time they got to the cages, Sam had personally petrified twenty-five of the horrible gits and they'd tied two sacks' worth of pebbles and left them leaning against the tunnel walls.

But the problem with having everything lit up was that the real horror of the cages was plain to see. Many of the children stood at the bars looking out at Sam and Gran. But some still sat at the rear, heads bowed, not even bothering to look up for fear that this was some new Dreable trick that was being played on them.

'Find Poppy,' Gran said to Sam.

He ran to the cages and began calling Poppy's name. She was in the middle tier right at the end.

'Sam? Sam?'

Sam heard his name and looked up.

'Sam? Is it really you?'

'Yeah,' said Sam. 'It's really me.'

Poppy's eyes drifted down to where Gran was muttering to herself as she struggled to find whatever she was looking for in the handbag.

'Is that…Is that Mother Merryweather?' asked Poppy in hushed tones.

'Yeah, that's her. I told you. She's my gran…'

He couldn't finish the sentence. Poppy suddenly yelled with triumph. 'Mother Merryweather. Mother Merryweather is here!'

It spread like wildfire through the cages. Children, terrorized by the dark and other worse things, suddenly began looking up. Sam saw the flaring of hope in eyes that had been dull and lifeless with despair. Gran came over and was all smiles for Poppy, who was holding her hands out through the bars. Gran reached up and took them and beamed.

'Mother Merryweather, you came,' Poppy said.

'Of course I did, Poppy. And you did well to call me. Your grandmother would be very, very proud of you. You are a real Keeper.'

Poppy's eyes shone.

'But now there's more work to be done,' Gran said. 'We have to get these children outside and into the park and eating. Can you do that, Poppy?'

'I think so,' Poppy said.

'Troop and Ginger will show you the way,' Gran said and glanced at the two animals. Troop barked and wagged his tail.

'But what about the cages?' Poppy said. 'They're all locked.'

Gran turned to Troop again. 'Find the keys, boy.'

The Labrador's tail went up and he started sniffing, covering the ground in a zig-zag pattern as he headed towards the far wall. Ninety seconds later they heard him bark. Sam ran over and saw Troop's tail wagging madly as he stood in front of a rickety ladder next to two sets of ancient rusting keys hanging on a wooden peg.

'Let Poppy out and then follow me. We have to get to the adults,' Gran said, and there was an urgency in her voice that Sam didn't much like. But he put the ladder against the cages and scrambled up to the door.

'I knew you'd come back,' Poppy said. 'I just knew it.'

'How did they get you?' Sam asked as he finally found a key that fitted the lock.

'One of them made itself into you. I should have known because there was no Troop or Ginger but the Dreable you said they were with your gran and...' She stopped, blinking away tears, and Sam felt another burst of anger at the thought that the Dreables had used him to trick her.

'Can you get them all out?' Sam asked, handing over the keys.

Poppy nodded and turned to some of the smaller children, who were becoming excited as they began to realise that this was most definitely not a Dreable trick. Sam went back down the ladder and helped some of the children down but then he heard Gran calling.

'Sam, it's time we went.'

'But Gran...'

'Listen,' she said.

Sam did. There was a lot of noise coming from the excited children. There was shouting and crying but beneath it all, Sam could hear something else.

'It's started,' said Gran and hurried off.

Sam followed. And as they left the clamour of the excited children behind, the noise became louder. There was no doubt about it now. Sam could hear the beating of drums.

Gran hesitated at the far end of the chamber. Here, the tunnel forked. She reached for the amber pendant around her neck and walked to the left tunnel, before retracing her steps to the right. Sam saw the pendant glow a golden yellow.

'This way,' she said.

Sam almost had to run to keep up with her. At every junction, she repeated the trick with the pendant. They met only a handful of Dreables and Gran let Sam deal with them. After a quarter of an hour of walking and consulting the pendant, Gran stopped quite suddenly. The thing was glowing much more brightly now, pulsing like a little sun in her hand. They were at a point in the tunnel where it opened out into a big alcove. Everywhere, the Skwarnok Aryon's light filled the space. As Gran stepped forward the alcove expanded into another huge chamber. From where they stood, ramps led down onto the floor of a huge cavern. But the floor of the cavern held a dreadful secret. At the far end four rows of bodies lay on the ground.

'Are they dead?' Sam shivered.

'No,' Gran said, and then added ominously, 'Not yet.'

And Sam saw that she was right. The village's adults lay with their eyes open, staring up at the craggy ceiling way above them. There were perhaps fifty Dreables in the chamber and none of them had seen Sam or Gran yet. Most of them were working ropes and pulleys so as to lift twenty or more of their kind up onto the ceiling, where they clung like bats from elaborate arrangements of ropes looped through crude metal staples. Some had huge picks strapped to their backs. Those that had attached themselves to the ceiling already wielded the picks in time to the rhythm. Sam suddenly realised what the drums were for.

'What are they doing?'

'They're opening up the chamber,' Gran said.

'To let in light?'

'No. They won't open it to the sky,' Gran explained before adding darkly, 'They'll open it to the earth above. They want to fill this chamber full of soil from the peat bogs over the roof.'

Sam glanced again at the ranks of people. 'But...'

He didn't have to finish. Gran did it for him. 'That's the way they make Dreables. Over time, a long time, the soil and Arglwd will change the people. They become one with it and from that mixture, the Dreables emerge.'

Sam made a face. From high above, one of the Dreables yelled triumphantly. Sam looked up to see it hit the ceiling with a mighty blow and send a shower of rocks and soggy black earth raining down.

'We have to stop this,' Gran said, looking around. 'If we could only get to the drums.'

Sam followed her gaze up to the wall to their right. There, on a ledge, stood a Dreable with his back to the chamber. He was beating time on two huge drums in front of a carved figure in the rock.

'Who is the statue?' Sam said.

'Arglwd,' Gran answered. 'Or what Arglwd once was.'

Sam stared. The figure was cloaked and wore a crown on its head. 'He looks like a king.'

'He was. But he forgot what a king should be. He lost

his wisdom and with it his people. Now he rules this empire of abominations. Damn.'

'What's the matter, Gran?'

'I don't think I can climb up there.' Gran was looking at the path to the ledge. It looked boulder strewn and treacherous.

'But I can,' Sam said.

'No, Sam, it's too...'

But Sam was already moving, picking his way across the floor. The climb wasn't difficult. Forty feet over a hill of scree? Nothing compared to where Mr and Mrs Jones often scrambled on an afternoon stroll in Snowdonia. Sam wasn't even out of breath as he crested the slope to the ledge. It was then he realised that the drummer was one of the biggest Dreables he'd seen; at least as big as the ones guarding Arglwd in the big hall. And worse, from this close the noise of the drums was almost deafening.

'Excuse me,' Sam yelled.

It was no good. The Dreable took no notice. Its huge shoulders worked as it beat at the two massive drums with sticks as big as fence posts. Every time it struck, the miners on the ceiling struck too, sending more earth down on the victims below. Sam knew he had to stop him, but how to get the thing's attention? He shuffled forward and suddenly, the answer was right there. Sam reached down and picked up a cricket-ball-sized stone. He was only a matter of a few feet away from the Dreable. Sam threw the stone as hard as he could. It hit the thing squarely between the big shoulder blades. The Dreable barely flinched and the stone clattered off as if it had hit something really hard and solid. But the rock did enough to make the drummer hesitate and glance behind. Sam waved his arms. The Dreable pivoted, swinging the huge drumstick around like a mace towards Sam. But Sam was ready. One glance was all it took.

'Bos Karrek!'

Despite the fact that the Dreable was twice the size of the average, the pebble that ended up on the floor was just the same as all the others. With the drums silent, Sam had expected that everything in the cavern might grind to a halt, but it was not to be. The pick handlers on the ceiling had their own rhythm now and didn't notice the lack of any beat.

Quickly, Sam grabbed one of the drumsticks and swung it at one of the drums. The force of the rebound almost sent him sprawling, but the second time he was more in control and after five incongruous beats he heard the knocking and hammering above come to a stuttering stop. He turned. Every Dreable in the cavern was looking at him. Snarls were beginning to rumble. But Sam was ready. He held out his hands, fingers splayed, just as the Dreables began to rush forward towards him in a wave.

'Talk to the hand,' Sam said and then quietly added, 'Bos Karrek.'

There was a clatter and rattle as fifty pebbles rolled

over the rough cavern floor. Sam looked up. The steady stream of sludgy brown-black earth from above dried to a trickle and was replaced by the rocky clatter of twenty shiny pebbles raining down.

Suddenly there was the sound of clapping. 'Oh, well done, Sam,' Gran yelled. Then she was moving across the cavern towards the sleeping adults. She brushed dirt and dust away from the faces of the first few and began putting tiny bits of Bakewell tart into their mouths. Within seconds, those that she'd fed were sitting up, blinking, and looking around in a daze.

But Gran seemed to be spending more time with one man in particular. She revived him and Sam could see her talking to him urgently. Gran made the introductions.

'Sam, this is Mr Jobson, parish councillor.'

Sam held out his hand and Mr Jobson shook it. He was a round man with a black moustache and sharp, intelligent eyes.

'Mr Jobson is going to help get everyone out.' Gran added.

Mr Jobson was already moving quickly amongst the others, doing exactly the same as Gran had done moments before, brushing off dirt and feeding the half-comatose people.

'Does he know the way out?' Sam asked.

'No, but you do.'

'Me?'

'Yes, you.'

'But...'

'Look for our footprints,' Gran urged. 'I've just got to sort myself out and get the rest of them awake,' she added, but she turned her back to Sam as she said it.

Sam didn't know what she meant about footprints until he was back in the tunnel. He hesitated at the first fork but studied the floor and saw, to his astonishment, two pairs of ghostly shimmering white footsteps clearly illuminated in the Silver Hare's light. Sam led the way, following his own backwards footprints, with Mr Jobson chivvying and encouraging the dazed villagers. Some of them had to be helped with walking and it took a lot longer to get out than it did coming in. When Sam felt fresh air on his face and saw the late evening light through the oval opening into the ring of standing stones, he stood to one side to allow the others to pass. They still looked shaken and shocked and they'd need more than a nibble of Mrs W's Bakewells. Sam remembered the special herb mixture Gran had added to the cookies and knew that it would be alright. It was then that the truth of it all finally struck him.

He'd assumed that because Gran didn't know about new stuff like video games and MTV that she was dull and pointless. He'd been wrong. So wrong that he could hardly believe it. All this time she'd known things about Dreables and Silver Hares and herbs that made bad things go away. All fantastic, amazing, important things. But he had just never bothered to listen.

As the last of the adults shambled by, Sam waited for

Gran, but she didn't appear. He called out her name and ran forward to look if she'd sneaked by in the crowd, but he could see no sign. Strange, he thought. He was sure she'd said for him to go first and she'd sort herself out and follow behind.

Sam thought about that. 'Sort myself out' could mean all sorts of things as far as Gran was concerned... Suddenly, Sam felt a pang of apprehension. He started walking back along the tunnel, but he'd only gone ten steps when a dreadful, mournful, spine-freezing roar rumbled out from deep in the Barrow. And then Sam knew what Gran had meant by sorting herself out.

She meant she needed to deal with unfinished business and by the sound of it, she'd found what she was looking for.

Arglwd.

THE BARGAIN

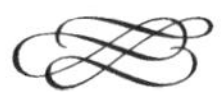

Sam ran back through the tunnels, this time following his ghostly footsteps the right way. He could see that the Skwarnok Aryon's light was just beginning to fade and shadows were creeping back into the alcoves. Darkness was reclaiming Arglwd's kingdom.

His heart was racing as he thundered down the tunnels, but Gran wasn't in the cavern where the Dreables had caged the children, nor was she in the burial chamber where Sam had pelted the drummer. But this was where he'd last seen her. Frantically, Sam searched the floor. His own ghostly white footsteps seemed to be everywhere. But then he heard a familiar noise. Ginger was meowing and prowling near a black tunnel opening in the far wall.

'Ginger, what are you doing here?' Sam crossed the soggy floor to where the cat stood watching him. As he reached down to stroke the cat's fur, he saw a set of glowing footprints in the tunnel.

Gran's.

The cat purred.

'Ginger, you're a star,' Sam said and set off down the tunnel, the noise of his own footfalls echoing in his ears. He headed away from the maze under the Barrows, and here, the Skwarnok Aryon's silver light had real difficulty penetrating. Sam's neck prickled the deeper he went and it took him a moment to realise why. He'd been here before.

Gran's footsteps were very faint now. Sam dabbed at his eyes, which watered from the stench of oily smoke from the flickering torches on the walls. But he didn't need their sickly light to know where he was.

The doors to the king's hall were open. The petrified statues loomed exactly as they had when Sam had been brought here, and he slipped in behind a particularly large one. When he peeked around it, the sight that greeted him froze the breath in his throat and he only just managed to stop himself from crying out. Gran was in the middle of the hall, flanked by the two huge Dreables that were Arglwd's personal guard.

The Dreable king stood in front of his throne at the very end with his back to Gran. But it was the Dreables that held Sam's attention. There was something about the way they held their heads, chins up, straining to hear or smell. One of them turned its head towards Sam and he ducked back into shadow. But not before he'd caught a glimpse of the Dreable's ugly face and its blind marble eyes.

He needed to get a bit closer. He flitted to the next statue and then on to another one. He was much closer to Gran now, almost opposite her. Gran was trying vainly to struggle out of the grasp of a huge Dreable hand, but it was no good.

'You can not run, cunning woman.' Arglwd's voice boomed out into the hall and broke the silence.

'Why don't you look at me, wiht?' Gran said.

'You think me a total fool?' rasped Arglwd. 'You want me to look so that you can curse me into another century of imprisonment and oblivion. You and your kind have meddled too much already. But I have had time to plan for your return. This time, I have an answer to your curses. My two faithful sightless pets have suffered gladly for their lord.'

Sam almost smacked his own head in realisation. Of course! That's why they were blind. Gran's Bos Karrek curse would be useless against them.

'Face me, coward,' Gran demanded, and there was a something in her voice that made Sam want to stand up and look at her so very much.

'You have taken back my spoils,' Arglwd hissed. 'But we will start again. I have nothing but time. And now you will be my guest as well. Know that I have prepared a very special place for you deep under the river. Take her.'

The Dreables moved. Gran was like a rag doll

between them. Sam waited until they'd left the hall and then as quietly as possible, he went after them. They travelled quickly, their blindness no impediment. The torches shed just enough light for Sam to follow. But ahead he could see that there was no more light. Deep in the Barrows the darkness beckoned and once in there, he would have no advantage. It was time to act.

'Wait,' Sam said.

The Dreables stopped, cocking their heads.

'What follows us?' demanded one.

'I am the ghost of the first Merryweather,' Sam said.

'Ghost?' asked the other Dreable.

'Merryweather?' repeated the second.

'Do you know who your prisoner is?' Sam asked,

'Cunning…' said the first.

'Woman…' said the second.

'Mother Merryweather,' said Sam.

'She can't harm us,' said Dreable one.

'We can't see her,' said Dreable two.

'But she is Mother Merrryweather,' said Sam. 'Mother Merryweather, understand? Mother Merryweather.'

'Mother…' said one.

'Merryweather…' said two.

'And I am a man,' Sam said.

'Man?' said the Dreables together.

'Can't you tell?'

'Tell?' repeated the Dreables.

Sam waited and then, crossing his fingers, he said,

'And all I want is a piece of cake.'

The Dreables frowned and hesitated. Even though they couldn't see, they seemed to look at one another in confusion but spoke as one. 'Piece of...?'

It was a silly thing to say, Sam knew. But not half as silly as the Dreables must have felt as the curse kicked in. There was a sudden crack in the air and they both imploded into two small pebbles that fell harmlessly to the floor.

Sam hurried forward and stood in front of his trembling grandmother.

'Poppy teach you that one?' she asked, grinning.

'Mother Merryweather's man-tell-piece,' Sam said and nodded.

Gran's eyes shone. 'She's a bright girl, that Poppy. Bright as a diamond, just like you.' She put her hand on Sam's head and brushed Dreable dust from his hair before turning back to face the way they came.

'How are we going to fight Arglwd, Gran?'

'We aren't going to fight him, Samm' Gran said gravely 'We've beaten him already. It's just that he doesn't want to admit it. Come on.'

Gran led the way. In the huge hall, Arglwd was sitting on his throne. His head didn't move but Sam saw the glint of his eyes as they looked up.

'You have allies, cunning woman. I should have known.'

'We are Merryweathers,' Gran said by way of an answer.

'Leave me, cunning woman. Let me fester here.'

'No,' said Gran. 'You can't be at peace. All that raving and hating. There is nothing for it.' She reached into her bag and took out two yellowed pieces of paper. The sight of them animated Arglwd. This time his head did come up, his face turning away from the little pieces of parchment in Gran's hands as if they were poison.

'Each time I learn,' he hissed, 'each time I learn a little more.'

But Gran ignored him. 'The old agreement still holds, and you are bound.' She held the parchments high in the air. In one movement, Gran crumpled the one in her right hand and with a crackle, it disintegrated in her fingers. 'Bos Karrek. Bos Tullwch,' she said clearly and loudly.

Arglwd reared up in his seat and roared. In that roar was anger and vengeance but it was nothing more than noise. His stretching body froze… and slowly, his petrified form began to crumble, the dust falling to the floor and finding its way into cracks and crevices so that within a minute there was nothing of him left but his throne.

'Where's he gone?' asked Sam.

'Back to the earth,' Gran said. She walked to Arglwd's stone seat. Beneath it was a dust-covered wooden box, about the size of the small jewellery box Sam's mum kept all her rings and earrings in. Carefully, Gran opened the box and laid the second piece of parchment inside.

'What's that for?' Sam asked.

'It's part of the agreement,' Gran explained. 'Arglwd sleeps and stays away from humans. But he only agreed to do that if we promise him a chance to wake again. On this piece of paper is written the incantation that will wake him. 'Gran saw Sam frown and smiled. 'No, it's not the same as those pot-holers found last week. It's different. It's always different.'

Sam looked down at the dust that was still shifting beneath his feet. 'But why don't you just get rid of him for good?' Sam asked.

Gran shook her head. 'He was here long before us, Sam. One day, when we're all gone, his kind might once again rule this land.'

'What about the box?'

Gran put the box back onto the floor under the throne. 'The box will find its way to somewhere away from prying eyes. But humans are curious creatures. Much worse than cats. Someone will find it eventually, but not for a very long time.'

Sam nodded. He sort of understood. It was like snakes and crocodiles. Just because he didn't like them it didn't mean they didn't have a right to live in jungles and swamps.

'What time is it, Sam?'

Sam looked at the luminous dial on his watch. 'Quarter to eight.'

'Excellent. Still plenty of daylight. Come on, we've got a party to get to.'

THE PARTY

The scene that greeted Sam and Gran as they emerged from the stone circle and through the stone archway into the park was so astonishing, that Sam couldn't stop a peal of delighted laughter from escaping his lips. Mr Jobson had organized a brass band and some people were dancing while squealing children played on the swings and the roundabout and chased each other in the late sunlight. The people of Wihtlea looked happy and carefree and Sam saw Gran's mouth form a smile of satisfaction.

Mr Jobson saw them, waved and hurried over.

'Has everyone eaten a cookie?' Gran asked.

'Two,' Mr Jobson said. 'Libby Brown brought some extras. So the whole village has eaten except me and Poppy Stevens,' he added, frowning.

'Well done, Mr Jobson,' said Gran. Sam couldn't help noticing the stark contrast between Mr Jobson's lined expression and dark-rimmed eyes and the glowing faces of those all around him. 'Your job is done. Go on, eat now,' Gran ordered.

Mr Jobson nodded and walked to the picnic table where Sam and Gran had laid out the cookies she'd baked earlier. Mr Jobson took one, but not before he glanced over towards the standing stones, as if he wanted one final reassurance that there was nothing nasty there.

'We're very, very grateful Mother Merryweather,' he said, the cookie inches from his mouth. 'If you hadn't come, I don't know what...' His hand started shaking so badly, he almost dropped the cake. Gran reached forward and held his wrist.

'Eat now,' she said softly. 'Just remember to seal all the potholes you can find.'

Mr Jobson nodded and bit into the biscuit. His face took on a puzzled expression as he chewed and then swallowed. 'Interesting taste,' he began. 'Bit of a mixture. Sweet and savoury and...sunshine and the sea on a calm day...and lambs gambolling on the hillside in spring...' His eyes lit up. It was as if someone had taken a cloth and wiped all the lines from his face and the darkness from under his eyes. Suddenly, his foot started tapping and he looked longingly across to the band. 'Right, if you'll excuse me, there's some dancing to be done.' He skipped towards the music, hand up, calling to his wife.

'What exactly did you put in those cakes, Gran?' Sam asked.

'Something to help people forget what they needn't remember,' Gran said.

'Am I going to forget?' Sam asked, not because he wanted to forget but because he was worried that Gran thought he ought to.

'No. It's your duty not to forget. And neither can Poppy.'

Even as she spoke, a girl with pigtails was running across the grass towards them. She ran straight at Gran and hugged her. She looked pale and tired. But Sam knew that she was also one of the bravest people he had ever met.

'Well, I think it's about time us three musketeers had something to cheer us up, don't you think?' Gran said. Poppy and Sam watched as Gran retrieved three intact cherry Bakewells from her handbag and handed one to each of them.

'You both deserve a medal,' Gran said, 'but it's the nature of our work that it remains unsung. Still, give me one of Mrs Walpole's Bakewells over a shiny badge any day of the week.'

Sam bit into the cake. Suddenly, the setting sun seemed brighter, the grass greener, and the tune the band was playing sounded like the most cheerful thing he'd ever heard. He looked up at the hills. They were green and unsullied by the Nule's grey blanket. Overhead, birds were beginning to return to their nests and everything looked almost back to normal. It was at that moment that the smell of cooking hit his nostrils.

'Hello, someone's set up a barbecue,' Gran said through a mouthful of cake. 'I smell sausages. Don't know about you, but I'm starving. Come on. Follow me. We are, after all, the guests of honour.'

Poppy watched Gwladys Merryweather striding across the park with shining eyes.

'Your gran is brilliant,' she said.

'Yeah,' Sam answered. 'I know.'

THREE DAYS later it was raining, and Sam was reading a book that Gran had given him. It was a very old book full of very interesting things. Sometimes he had to ask Gran what some of the words meant, but he was managing. He was so engrossed in a chapter on mountain trolls and how they hated baked beans that he didn't even hear the car. In fact, the only clue he had that his parents had arrived back to collect him was the sound of his dad's voice calling to him from the hallway. He stuck in the bookmark Gran had given him and ran down the stairs. There was the usual round of hugs and dad ruffling his hair and comments like, 'I swear you've grown another inch,' before they settled down in Gran's living room to swap stories.

Mum and Dad's were full of words like 'vistas' and 'high passes,' but Sam only really tuned in when they started talking about the strange fog they'd come across that had rolled in completely out of the blue and left them stranded for half a day. But all in all they'd had a great time.

'And,' said his mum with a glance at his dad, 'we met this guide who's running a special trip to Switzerland and guess what? He says there's room for us at half term and,' she paused for effect, 'he says that you can come too.'

Sam looked into her excited eyes. 'You mean me?'

'Of course you,' Mum said. 'No more leaving you out, Sam. Your dad and I have talked a lot and – well, if you find it too hard we can always let you stay in the hotel, which is a really nice one and – '

'But I usually come to Gran's,' Sam said.

'Yeah,' said his dad, 'and I know how much of a pain that's been so – '

'No,' yelled Sam. 'I can't come with you. I mean Gran and me…we…'

His mother and father were staring at him with very quizzical expressions.

'…Gran and me have got some trips planned,' Sam explained and swallowed hard.

'Are you serious?' Dad asked.

At that moment Gran entered with a tray laden with cups and the usual mountainous supply of home-baked cakes.

'Serious about what?' Gran asked.

'About you and Sam planning trips together?' Mum asked.

Gran looked from Sam's pleading face to his mother and father's confused expressions.

'Is there a problem?' Gran said.

'October,' Mum said. 'We thought we'd go for a fortnight at half term. Sam will lose a week of school but it's such a great deal…'

'Ah, half term,' Gran said, nodding. 'Yes. Unfortunately, Sam and I are visiting an old friend in the Scottish Highlands over half term. She was in my cookery class at school.'

'That sounds nice,' said Mr Jones with a fixed smile.

'Sounds brilliant,' Sam said.

'Since when were you so keen on cooking?' his dad asked with eyebrows up near his hair line.

'I'm learning,' Sam protested.

'So,' said his mother, sensing an opportunity which was too good to miss, 'you don't mind if we go?'

'Bit of fresh air will do you good,' Sam said, trying to not make it sound too much like the way his mother kept telling him the exact same thing. 'By the way, the cakes you're eating are mine.'

His mother, who had just taken a sip of tea, promptly sprayed most of it over his father's shirt.

'Yours?' she spluttered. 'But…but they're…good.'

'I call them karreck cakes,' Sam said, beaming at them.

Gran sent him a warning look.

'Unusual name,' his dad said as he took a bite and his

eyes became very large. 'Though I have to admit, they are pretty darn good.'

'So, apart from learning how to make very good cakes,' his mother said as she took a second bite of hers, 'what else did you and Gran get up to?'

'Oh, the usual,' said Sam. 'Pottered about. Met some people, visited some caves, you know.'

'Caves, really? Were they spooky?' Dad asked.

'Nah,' Sam said. 'Anyway, I want to hear about your trails.'

He didn't really, but once they got on to those, they'd forget all about wanting to know what he and Gran did. Out of the corner of his eye, he saw his gran smiling. But his mother wasn't quite ready to be deflected so easily.

'Mum,' she said to Gran earnestly. 'You're sure about this half term trip? I don't want Sam to be a burden. I mean what on earth will there be to do in Scotland for the two of you?'

'Oh, there'll be plenty to do,' Gran said. 'Bertha says something's stealing her chickens and reckons it might be a Bodach infestation. By the time we get that sorted out, there'll be no time to be bored.'

Silence, like a three-hundredweight lead blanket, fell on the living room. No one quite knew what to say next. So Sam jumped right in.

'So what about the walk in the high pass, was it fun?'

'It was brilliant,' said his dad.

His mother sent a long suspicious look between Sam

and Gran, but then she shrugged. 'The trip was totally amazing,' she said finally. 'Look, we've taken loads of pictures.'

Sam looked at the photos and asked a couple of enthusiastic questions as they flicked through endless pictures of scenery and trails. In each one of them his mum and dad looked sweaty but very happy. They told stories of cheeky squirrels and Aztec sacrificial sites and after a while, Sam realised that he and Gran might as well not be there at all, so lost in reminiscences were his parents. But he didn't mind. He wasn't really listening to them anyway. He was too busy wondering if Gran really did have a friend called Bertha in the Highlands. He glanced across at her questioningly, but she was biting into another cake. Yet, he couldn't help but notice that the twinkle was very much back in her eye.

'More tea anyone?' said Gran lifting the teapot.

'Yes, please,' Dad said.

'I'll do it,' Sam said. 'I don't mind.'

'I didn't know you could make tea,' said Sam's mother, watching him take the teapot out to the kitchen.

'Oh, I've learned loads of stuff this holiday,' Sam said over his shoulder. 'You'd be surprised.'

He heard Gran splutter as she choked on a bit of cake, but he didn't look around. Troop and Ginger sat in the kitchen. They looked up as he walked in.

'I expect you already know what a Bodach is and how to get rid of it,' he whispered.

Troop wagged his tail and Ginger purred deep in his throat.

* * *

Holidays with Gran.

A week ago he would have done anything to avoid one.

Now, he'd already worked out that there were only nine weeks, three days, and five hours until the next one.

He smiled to himself and began filling up the kettle so that he could make another pot of Sam Jones tea for his yomping parents.

The End

THANK YOU

Thank you for reading *The Curse of Wihtlea barrows.* #1 in the Merrryweathers Mysteries. Please let me know if you enjoyed it. Keeping in touch with readers is one of the things I love about being a writer, and so I like to send out details of new releases, special offers and news relating to the series to those who are interested.

You can sign up at;
www.smarturl.it/RhysAJonesauthorpage

IF YOU ENJOYED THE RIDE, WHY NOT HELP SPREAD THE WORD

Authors still live and die by word of mouth. Honest reviews by genuine and loyal readers help bring the books to the attention of others.

Please feel free to Jump right in and leave a review wherever you bought this book –it can be as short as you like on the book's Amazon page.

OTHER BOOKS IN THE SERIES

The Curse of Borage Doone.

The trouble begins when Sam's Granny Merry-weather wins a competition set by her favourite TV chef, and she's over the moon. But things aren't at all what they seem when it comes to prize-giving. There are things wandering Edinburgh's dark alleys that would love to turn Sam into their dish of the day. Old grudges surface and Sam's growing knowledge of the cunning ways is about to be severely tested. But what he doesn't realise is that there's a much bigger prize at stake...The Curse of Borage-Doone.

You can find out more at: www.jonestheauthor.com

The Curse of Ragman's Hollow

Instead of Sam spending a holiday with granny Merryweather so that he can finish his braintrilloquism exam, he's off for a week to a remote cottage (Mum's suggestion) where nettle soup, NMP (No mobile phone) and long walks are the rule. Hesta Hollinghurst is in charge and she believes in foraging for food and ignoring warnings. So, it's no surprise that she insists on visiting Ragman's hollow, a place that the locals avoid like the plague. But there is no smoke without fire and soon it's obvious that whatever lurks in that desolate place has plans of its own for any visitors. When Sam's mother disappears and the Hollnghursts start eating raw sausages, there's something badly amiss. Sam finds himself up against an old and very tricky enemy. He's going to need every ounce of his cunning to stop the Ragman, but can he do it alone?

You can find out more at: www.jonestheauthor.com